I0541156

Heavy Mascara

and
Other Stories of Crime and Deception

CATHY ANN ROGERS

Aquitaine Ltd
Phoenix, Arizona

Previously published stories have been revised or modified from their
original versions as noted.

"The Usual" by Cathy Rogers. Original version first published in *Wizard of
Words Anthology 2009 Edition.* Copyright © 2009.

"The Protector" by Cathy Rogers. Original version first published on *Twist of
Noir* available at http://a-twist-of-noir.blogspot.com. Copyright © 2010.

"The Night Out" by Cathy Rogers. Original version first published on
Mysterical-e available at http://mystericale.com. Copyright © 2010.

"Spiked Heels" by Cathy Rogers. Original version first published in *The Path
Magazine, Book One.* Copyright © 2011.

"Woman's Work" by Cathy Ann Rogers. First published in *SoWest Crime
Time.* Copyright © 2013.

This is a work of fiction. Names, characters, businesses, places, events and
incidents are either the products of the author's imagination or used in a
fictitious manner. Any resemblance to actual persons, living or dead, or
actual events is purely coincidental.

Sally J Smith, Editor
Cover design by JD Smith Designs

Copyright © 2014 Cathy Ann Rogers

All rights reserved. This book or any portion thereof may not be reproduced
or used in any manner whatsoever without the express written permission of
the publisher except for the use of brief quotations in a book review.

All rights reserved.

ISBN: 0-9914843-6-3
ISBN-13: 978-0-9914843-6-2

www.aquitaineltd.com

NOTE FROM THE AUTHOR

I wrote many of these stories over the years, but left them mainly unfinished until I brought them out of the trunk recently. With the help of my editor, I brought them to the twenty-first century and have given them life at last.

TABLE OF CONTENTS

HEAVY MASCARA

Leah studied Tommy's face from across the table. A faint breeze drifted through the open window and ruffled her fine arm hairs. Cincinnati's Fore and Aft Restaurant, known as the first floating restaurant neatly tucked away on the Ohio River shoreline, rocked gently against the water's edge, a rhythmic tapping against the dock that was both hypnotic and soothing. Wet air swelled the dining room walls of the converted barge, leaving her clothes hanging limp against her skin in the August humidity. She turned away from him to watch the soft lights bounce off the river's glassy surface distorted by intermittent subtle undercurrents. When she turned her gaze back inside, she sensed doom that caused her to shiver. The candle glow between them created flickering silhouettes against the darkened window that unnerved her.

Tommy extended his hands across the table to cover hers. "Be fair," he said.

"Fairness is not an option," Leah said. She raised a manicured finger to follow the outline of her lips to smooth her lipstick.

Movement behind the partition that separated their table from their neighbor seemed to distract him. She saw his quick

1

sideways glance and gave his hand a squeeze.

"Come on, Leah. You've changed in a short time. Tell me what's happened."

She fixed him with a stare, and said, "Tommy, it's your work. I'm afraid being with you puts me in danger."

"Keep it down. Someone might hear you. Where do you get these delusions, anyway? Who's been filling your head with this nonsense?"

"Nobody. I can figure stuff out on my own."

Tommy bowed his head in surrender. The "Garibaldi Tool and Die Company" is like any other legitimate small business. Nothing dangerous or mysterious. Makes me wonder what's happened in your past that you see gangsters around every corner. I'm tired of having this conversation. Let's eat and try to have a nice meal for a change. Here, have more wine and relax," he said. He raised the wine carafe, and leaned toward her to fill her glass.

Leah avoided his penetrating glare. "I've got to see the ladies room," she said.

Tommy took a large gulp of wine and stared ahead. He considered himself good at keeping his temper, but this woman took him to his limits. This relationship had stopped being fun. He knew the time had come to end it, but dreaded the big scene. He poured more wine, drank his glass empty, and motioned the waiter for another bottle. He wondered what took her so long, and then realized that he did not really miss her.

Noises from behind the partition next to Tommy interrupted the silence he had been enjoying. A soft female whine, a deep male voice quieting her, and then silence. Bare skin skidded across the vinyl seat behind him, followed by the draw of air from a fast moving body passing by. His eyes rested on her diminutive feminine figure when she came into his peripheral view. Concerned, but not curious enough, he inhaled and looked forward to an end to this evening.

Leah soaked in the atmosphere of the narrow anteroom in the ladies lounge. Walls swathed in subtle hues of pink and beige conveyed a feminine calm. Her eyes moved to a white leather sofa, a black marble vanity contrasted by cushioned white vanity benches—the sterility a surprising elegance. She had leaned into her reflection to smooth out the creases of her eye shadow, when she heard the swoosh of the swinging door.

When she looked up to see who had come in, Leah noticed a young girl paused just inside the doorway, staring at her. "What?"

"The way you outline your eyes with that thick layer of eyeliner and heavy black mascara is so cool. How do you get that off every night?"

"Thanks for the compliment," Leah said, and gave the girl a smug grin before turning back to the mirror.

"I'm Carol," she said. "Do you come here often? This is my first time here and I think it's lovely." When Leah did not answer, she said, "Are you from around here? Is that your husband sitting with you? Do you live around here?"

Leah turned around to face her. "What's with all the questions?" Leah had perfected a deep masculine voice intended to intimidate and she saw it had the intended effect. Carol turned to leave, but Leah called out, "Did you only come in here to spy on me?"

"I wasn't spying. I'm sorry." Carol flushed, and then scurried past Leah through the heavy wooden door to the stalls.

Leah decided not to bother checking the rest of her face, and rushed out to the dining room. She had to calm herself to keep a natural pace when she came back into view of the other patrons. That girl set her on edge. She had an eerie, waif-like character that reminded her of a living ghost.

Tommy watched Leah approach their table. Sleek and lithe, but now with an uncharacteristic urgency in her movements. She sat down, looked behind her, and took a deep breath.

Careful not to let her draw him into another one of her fantasies, he took a sip of wine and watched her. She replaced the napkin on her lap and seemed relieved. She took up her wine glass, tipped it to her mouth, and looked at him.

"Anything wrong?"

"No. Why would there *be*? I only went to the bathroom."

"So this is how it's going to be every time we go out to dinner? You pout while I sit across from you wondering what's going on with you."

"Let's just eat and get this meal over. I don't like it here anymore."

Neither spoke more than small talk during the rest of the meal. During the ride home, he considered the silence healing and a time for reflection. The more they argued, the more he regretted proposing to Leah after only knowing her six months. After years of cautious observation of women, he thought he had acquired an ability to recognize authenticity. Until now.

Once they were home, he switched on the television in the bedroom for the news, or maybe more for the distraction. Leah appeared in the bedroom doorway a few minutes later. She posed there as she often did, waiting for an invitation to interrupt. His cynical nature told him that was more an act than a courtesy. When he did not respond, she crossed the room, and sat next to him on the bed.

"I've got to talk about what happened at the restaurant, I mean, in the bathroom."

He drew a breath, and exhaled. *Now what.* "What happened?"

"This scruffy girl came in. First, she stands there staring at me. I called her on it, so then she started asking me all kinds of questions. I know she came in to watch me. She wasn't interested in doing anything else in there. I left in a hurry. What do you think that was all about?"

Tommy tried to follow her conversation and listen to the news. He offered the obligatory comment, "I don't know. Why does it have to mean anything? She sounds socially awkward.

So what?"

"Well, I thought we were being watched by one of your underworld figures. I've heard of these things but I never dreamed it would happen to me."

"Don't be ridiculous, Leah," he said. "Sometimes situations appear sinister when they're not. Stop creating drama where none exists. I think you're addicted to chaos. You're not satisfied unless something's wrong."

"Well, all I have to say is this. If someone's after you, I hope you think to keep me safe." Leah stood in front of him, blocking his view of the screen, hands on her hips.

"I'm getting to my limit with this crap." The ringing telephone cut him off. Tommy leaned over and answered it. "Hello.... What?...You're kidding... Did you call the police... I see.... Who was she... I'll tell her. What did the officer say... Yeah, it's upsetting. Thanks for taking care of the situation. I'm glad you're on duty.... I'll talk to you tomorrow, Marvin." Tommy replaced the receiver and looked at Leah. She had moved to sit beside him again, waiting in eager anticipation.

"What was that all about?"

"Marvin said a girl came in looking for you. He told her she had the wrong address. He hopes you're not angry about that, but he didn't think she looked like someone you would know. His words, not mine. She kept insisting you were here and when she wouldn't leave, he had no choice but to call the police."

"What did she look like?"

"Thin and pale with dark blond hair piled on her head, blue blouse, and black tights. Does this sound familiar to you?"

"Yes!" Leah said. She jumped up, waving her finger at Tommy. "That's the girl in the restaurant. I knew it. She *was* spying on me. She and the rest of the gang are going to get me. Oh, my God." The pitch of Leah's voice climbed higher with each word. She ran her hands through her thick dark hair. Her eyes moved between the patio door and the living room. "Can we get out through the patio?"

Tommy looked at her, alarmed more by her behavior than

by any potential threat. "Calm down," Tommy said. "I doubt she's part of anything as melodramatic as you imagine." He reached over for her, put his arms around her waist until she fell into him and rested her head on his shoulder. "I don't know what it's all about, but we'll figure it out. Don't worry."

She sniffled, and said, "Okay."

The morning sun beamed through the slats of the shuttered windows and fell across their faces. Leah yawned and stretched her arms and legs, while Tommy watched the light play against the bare walls. He rolled over to rest his arm around her waist, enjoying her softness against his bare skin.

"Good morning," he said. "It's eight o'clock and time to get up."

"What time did we get to sleep last night? I don't feel like I've slept at all," Leah said. A ray of light reached her face and she instinctively raised her hand to shield her eyes.

"Four thirty."

Leah groaned. "I'll make the coffee. You get the paper?"

"I'll make breakfast." Tommy winked, grinning at her as he found the fleshy part of her waist and tried to tickle her. She jumped out of bed before he had the chance and ran into the kitchen giggling.

While he pulled out the ingredients for the omelet, he sneaked glances as she prepared the coffee. The same fretful expression of the night before had returned, but he decided to leave it alone. Maybe she had a reason to worry that had nothing to do with him and her paranoia about the mob. He knew only the highlights of her life—the facts she wanted him to know—*she* could be the one with a dark past.

"I think I'll take a quick shower," she said. "I won't be long."

Tommy enjoyed watching her walk away. The sensual movements of her hips swaying in rhythm with her long hair, and poised hands had the elegance of a dancer. For the first time, he questioned his feelings, wondering if he was in love with the woman or her naked sexuality.

Leah stood in front of the vanity mirror studying her face. She ran a fingertip over the stale eye makeup she had not removed the night before. She closed her eyes to massage her eyelids swollen from the heavy layers of mascara that poked into the fleshy underlids like plastic shards as she slept. She jumped when Tommy walked up behind her.

"Feeling better today," he said.

She turned around, wrapped her arms around his waist, and buried her face into his chest.

"I'm scared."

"No one's going to hurt you while I'm around. Trust me."

She gave a half laugh, and said, "Trust me? I think the *Manliness for Dummies Manual* needs to come up with a new line."

"Ok. Believe in me. Better? Hey, forget the shower. Sit with me and have a cup of coffee while I finish the omelets."

"Did you bring in the paper yet?"

"No, I forgot," he said. "Can you run out and get it?"

"Sure, I'll be right back." She gave him another hug, and headed down the hallway to the front door. She opened the door, and called back to him, "Paper's not here. I'll go down and get a copy from Marvin."

Tommy inhaled the aroma of the brewing coffee while he got on with his cooking. He started the cooking to impress her but realized the therapeutic effect the rhythm of cooking had on him. He folded the omelet and peeked at the buttered bagel halves toasting under the broiler, his timing perfected. Then the telephone rang.

"Yeah," Tommy said impatiently.

"You don't know me, but I know you. I know a lot about you," a male voice said.

"What?" Tommy said. "Who is this? I hear you making

noise but not making sense."

"I know about you. I know about your family. I know about your business. What I know, you don't want to go public. Need I say more? I'll keep it simple. I have the proof. So, if you want me to go away, I want a hundred and fifty thousand dollars. Ignore me and I'm going straight to the cops. Have your answer by five today."

Dead air followed a click. He stared at the phone with squinted his eyes, hoping to see the caller's name or number. Nothing.

Black smoke swirled from the edges of the oven door. The burnt bagels and the omelet, now dry and slick, were beyond eating. He pulled the skillet from the stovetop and flung it into the sink. In another quick movement, he lifted the bagels from the broiler and flung them in the same direction. He gave into his rage with a solid punch to the wall. The cabinet doors shook, glasses tinkled. He regretted the burning pain on his knuckled.

"My God," Leah said. "What happened? Who was that on the phone?" He had not heard her return and regretted his loss of control.

"Someone who's going to wish they never found my number."

"Who?"

Her presence reminded him to stay calm. After the lobby incident last night, she would have all the confirmation that she needed that someone wanted to hurt her if she knew about the threatening phone call.

"Nothing really. I hate telemarketers, that's all."

"A little warning next time. You're frightening sometimes."

Be natural. Don't look concerned.

Later in the shower, Tommy embraced the hot water pelting his face and shoulders as he reran the caller's words. Tommy believed that anyone believing he would give into extortion had no idea of his real danger. He did not believe in suspicious coincidences, and he doubted that either the call or the visit downstairs last night by the same girl who approached

Leah at the restaurant were random or isolated—more like converging episodes.

Tommy stopped at the lobby desk, surprised to see Marvin, the concierge on duty last night. He sipped coffee and sorted mail for vacationing tenants, until Tommy tapped on the counter to get his attention. He looked up, ready to say something until the vintage switchboard buzzed. Marvin held up his finger signaling he would be right with him.

Tommy leaned against the chest high counter that separated Marvin's domain from the rest of the lobby. The inner sanctum was neat, organized, and polished with small pictures of tiny people Tommy recognized as Marvin's children and grandchildren. The display gave Tommy the impression that Marvin preferred to remember his children as they were in the past instead of as aging adults.

"I'll take care of it for you, Mrs. Radcliff. Go on your vacation and don't give your cat or plants another thought." He disconnected the call, and swung around the switchboard, but remained seated.

"Good morning, Mr. Garibaldi. Crazy down here last night. Course, after that weird broad left, things calmed down. A few tenants heard about the commotion and complained. I said, "you can't avoid the rest of the world all the time.""

Tommy thought it ironic Marvin did not consider himself part of the rest of the world.

"Here's the thing, see. I heard the officers talking. She's a regular downtown. Gets her boyfriend or husband out of jail often enough. They didn't say why *he* was in jail, but probably drugs."

Marvin shook his balding head, "Shame really. She's got the makings to be a real beauty. Shame what people do to themselves."

"Yeah, real shame," Tommy said. "So they arrested her?"

"Disturbing the peace. Yep, she's another lost child."

"What would we do without you," Tommy said, and slipped a fifty into Marvin's palm.

"Thank you, sir." Marvin smiled, and pushed the button to

open the garage entrance.

Tommy drove down Clifton Avenue North to the house where he had lived most of his life. He warmed at the sight of the Sycamore trees and hedges that shielded the house from traffic and noise. He drove along the driveway past the flower borders to the circular driveway and stopped at the front door. The warmth that embraced him came from memories of a time when the yellow two-story house had been home to six children, two Ukrainian sheepdogs, two parents, and periodic visiting relatives from overseas. Returning home reminded him of how lucky he was to have been born into this family.

"Your father said you were coming by," his mother said, wrapping her chunky arms around him, and kissing both cheeks. "Come in. What can I get you? Tea, coffee?"

His mother had generous warmth he found lacking in women his own age. When he complained about it, she graciously and charitably pointed out that young women needed time to develop into mature qualities. *Sure, Mom.* He knew from the family that she had possessed that tenderness all her life. The love he felt when she greeted him on his visits made the problems of the world inconsequential and her home a retreat. The idea she would be gone one day upset him more with the passing of time.

"Nothing right now, thanks, Mom. Is Dad in his office? I need to talk to him about something."

"He was in the den the last time I looked. I've been in the kitchen. Let's go see," she said. She took his hand leading him down the wide hallway. "Have you eaten this morning? I can make something?"

"I *am* hungry."

They stopped at the closed den door. She opened it wide and motioned him into the room. "Go on in. Poppa, Tommy's here to see you. Then I feed him."

Giuseppe Garibaldi stood up to greet him. "I'm pleased to see you, Son. Have a seat." A broad hand, toughened but manicured, gestured Tommy to the visitor's chair.

"I'll be back with coffee and *cornettos*," Mrs. Garibaldi said and closed the door behind her.

"Tommy, when I look at you, I see history in front of me. Our ancestors were men of purpose, patriots, adventurers, unifiers. The first Giuseppe Garibaldi nicknamed the *Hero of Two Worlds* for his military expeditions in South America and Europe and for his efforts in the formation of a unified Italy. His son, Giuseppe Garibaldi, Jr., fought under Pancho Villa and Francisco Madera as a Lieutenant Colonel in the anti-relectionist army of the 1910 Mexican Revolution. I see in you the same vitality and call to action. You're brave, loyal, and intelligent. I'm a fortunate man to have not one good son, but three, and daughters who can stand next to any of you with the same convictions and dedications"

Tommy frowned, confused by the sudden accolades out of sync in a small intimate meeting. "Thank you, Dad. I value your opinion of me."

"Our family reputation is important to me. I wouldn't want anyone to come into this family that was less than honest. I don't make a habit of sticking my nose in your affairs, but I'm making an exception. It's about Leah."

"Leah?"

"Yesterday, our delivery driver, Ryan, saw her sitting with a disreputable fellow in the Coffee House restaurant downtown. When Leah saw him, she rushed over and explained that the place was crowded when she arrived and the man offered to share his table with her. Ryan had no reason to doubt her until she stuck two fifty dollar bills in his shirt pocket and asked him not to mention he'd seen her. He returned the money and said 'no thanks.' After his wife left him for another man, he has no tolerance for cheaters. He called me as soon as he got in his van."

The old man leaned back in his chair.

"There's something going on, Dad. That's why I wanted to talk to you in private. It might be related."

"Well, son, let's hear it."

Tommy raised his head and looked at his father the same way he remembered doing as a child—no embellishments, no emotions, just the events since from last evening at the restaurant to the phone call this morning. When he finished, he leaned back into his chair with eyes closed, suddenly exhausted and anxious. "And all this talk about our family's mob connections wears me out."

"You didn't mention the true nature of the call to Leah, then?"

"No. I didn't see a reason to upset her after last night. I can handle a petty blackmailer."

"I take it you haven't told her the truth about what you do?"

"No," Tommy said. "I plan to before we're married. The fewer people who know, the better. Maybe I've been putting it off because I'm not sure we're a hundred percent about each other."

"But she already believes she's put two and two together about you, not knowing she came up with five. What if she repeated that conclusion to someone else, like this man she met?"

"That's crossed my mind," Tommy said. He shook his head. "But I don't want to accuse her if I'm wrong. That's why I intend to take care of this on my own without official involvement until I have more facts."

"In that case, find out if the coffee shop has video surveillance cameras. Ask around about the girl Carol. You can use the private investigator we used in the embezzlement case at the office. He's discrete. We can't be sure the blackmail has anything to do with Leah until we identify the blackmailer. Or until we find out the blackmailer is the man she met."

Tommy fixed his stare on the monkey bars outside the window, and felt grounded in the memories of childhood.

"You're in control, son, and you're not alone. Master your feelings. Emotions cloud judgment and that's dangerous."

Giuseppe stood and walked over to meet Tommy at the door. "Now go, but make sure you let your mother make you a takeaway sack with a coffee. Call me if you need me."

Tommy walked out the front door beyond the security and stability of his childhood into the perils of emotional trap doors. How many more lessons did he have in front of him before he grew into the man his father was?

He placed his coffee in a holder, reached inside his glove compartment to touch his Glock for reassurance before driving away. At the corner of Clifton and Ludlow Avenues, he pulled over at the alert on his tablet to read the information sent. He typed the address into the GPS and drove to the Over-The-Rhine district.

North of downtown Cincinnati, the Over-The-Rhine neighborhood, once a thriving business district of successful breweries and beer gardens, had declined to one of "America's poorest, most run-down neighborhoods" to the "largest, most intact urban historic district in the United States." A new energy, a combination of historical reverence and an eye for commercial opportunity evolved into revitalization a few years ago that brought back its respectability and its economic potential.

Tommy's parents' history had been like other immigrants who came to Cincinnati with little more than strong work ethics, and an ambition to succeed in what they undertook. He considered himself a part of their world—the hardworking middleclass opening corner grocery stores, Finley Market, and ethnic restaurants. All seemed to be long-forgotten local history by most until the recent revival by people devoted to cultural preservation.

Tommy turned onto one of the last streets not yet rehabilitated, and slowed while he searched for the right address. The apartment building, deteriorated and squalid, almost looked abandoned. Dirty children played on the steps, smearing dirty hands on the door handle and each other, and running away grunting and yelling incomprehensible sounds. An attractive black woman bulging with the impatience of new birth hollered to control the children but ended up looking ineffectual and defeated as they ignored her and ran down the street. She looked after them, angry at first, but he saw the beginnings of tears in her eyes. When she realized Tommy was looking at her, her face stiffened and she turned to walk up the concrete stairs.

"Excuse me, ma'am. Does Carol Thor live here?"

She surveyed him with narrowed eyes, and said, "Who wants to know?"

"I'm a friend of hers. I heard about last night and thought I'd stop by to see if she's okay."

The woman continued to study him for several seconds, and then her hard and impenetrable frown softened into a broad smile. "She's up there. Third floor, turn right, second door. By the way, I don't believe you're a friend of hers, but neither am I."

He saw the dark, rickety stairs of the decaying foyer and started to move toward them when the putrid smell coming from the row of garbage cans lined up next to the wall hit his throat. Tommy held his breath while he walked up the stairs to the third floor. By the time he reached the third floor landing, he breathed easier with tiny breaths, but the memory of stench stayed with him.

Tommy knocked. He leaned his ear in to listen and heard a creaking sound inside. When no one answered, he knocked a second time, hard. The door must have been unlatched, because it swung inward. He stuck his head inside and called out, "Carol. Carol Thor."

He heard her before he saw her, a low, groggy voice coming from a sofa facing away from the door and toward the window beyond. A hand reached up to grab the back of the sofa. When he saw her, his jaw dropped. She looked worse than what he had imagined. He did not recognize her as anyone he saw at the restaurant.

"Carol, my name is Tommy. I'd like to ask you a few questions about last night. It's important. Are you up to it?"

Carol tried to focus her half-opened eyes, but fell backward. Tommy entered the room, his eyes moving left to right for signs anyone else was there. When he assured himself they were alone, he moved in closer. He looked down at her, lying in an awkward pose, eyes fluttering. She might have been fading in and out of consciousness. The idea of calling an ambulance occurred to him until she started talking.

"What do you want to know? I made an ass out of myself, got arrested, and went to jail. The only thing worse than that is telling strangers about it. Is that what you want to know?"

"No. I want to know why you were there and how you know Leah. Don't tell me you don't know her. You wouldn't have had reason to watch her, if you didn't."

Tommy walked around to the front of the sofa to find a place to sit. She had a soiled white sheet draped around her, but nothing else. What might have been provocative neither aroused him or impressed him. Her body looked tired, out of shape, and roughly sculpted. He saw a thinning cotton robe draped over the coffee table and tossed it to her. "Put this on while we talk."

"I don't want to talk. I want to be alone. Come back some other time."

"I want to talk now. It's important."

He saw her react to the sudden sharpness in his voice. She sat up, reached for the robe, and pulled her arms through the sleeves. She reached for a cigarette, but put it back without lighting it.

"If you must know, I was looking for the bitch that's been running around with my boyfriend." She paused when she saw his surprise.

"What's his name?" Tommy forced down an eruption of rage.

"Robert Harleton."

He typed a note on his cell phone. She leaned over to see what Tommy wrote, and then spelled out the last name. "Okay. Go on."

"We went to the restaurant together, but he left right after you. I thought he went to meet her somewhere. I knew where she lived, so I went there to see if could catch them together. At least confront her. That old guy overreacted. I wasn't threatening him."

"Why would you think Robert would be with Leah? What connection is there between them?"

Carol sobered as she realized the gravity of the information she was telling him. She moved her tongue over chapped lips.

"Why should I help you? Maybe I tell you all I know and you kill him. Then where am I? I'm pregnant. I need a roof over my head. I'd be crazy to cut myself off from what I know is a sure thing to do you a favor. Me, walk out into the world with no job, no place to live, and no friends. What's in it for me?"

Tommy watched her looking at him, She seemed defiant and fearful manner, and perhaps a little proud.

"Carol, look, I'm going to be straight. Someone's trying to blackmail me."

"Yeah."

"You and Robert have become involved in my life in the past twenty-four hours. I'm not sure why or how, but I need to know how this connects to Leah. I said before, that you don't have to talk to me, but maybe I'll make it worth your trouble if you will."

"How?"

"You want to get out of here into a decent place and have your baby in good environment, right?"

She nodded and he continued.

"I have a couple apartment buildings. I also have a business. What about an apartment and a job in exchange for all I want to know?"

Carol eyed him as he had done her moments before. "Are you for real? Why should I believe you? How do I know you mean what you say? That you won't take what I say and disappear."

"Get dressed."

Carol gave him a questioning look.

"Go ahead," he said. "Get dressed and I'll take you to the apartment. I'll prove it to you. If you're serious about leaving, that is. I'll wait for you to get your things together. Your information is important to me and I'm willing to pay for what you know."

Carol turned her head and eyed him speculatively then. She got up and went into the tiny bathroom. When she returned, she looked fresh with a clean face, and her hair pulled back into a French twist. She wore jeans, a peasant blouse, and tennis shoes. A little of the desperation in her demeanor had been replaced with a glow of hope.

A deep sadness rushed over him knowing all the people who lived like this their entire lives without hope. He thought about his parents' house where he grew up and how different his life would be had they lived here. He knew then he would have helped her whether she talked or not. This was no environment to bring a baby into the world.

He was as eager to escape this building as he was to find out what she knew. They moved down the stairs and through the front door. Tommy took his first deep breath since leaving her apartment and hoped she did not notice.

Carol remained vigilant and silent during the drive. As the car proceeded north into the cleaner streets, well-manicured lawns, and newer model cars, Tommy noticed her vigilance turn to anticipation. When he pulled up in front of a four-family apartment building in College Hill, she looked over to him and said, "This is it? This is nice. It's yours?"

"I bought it a few years ago as an investment. It pays for itself," Tommy said, embarrassed at the disparity of their circumstances. "Let's go up."

He opened his door, went around to open hers and they went inside. Tommy unlocked the security door that led into the hallway on the first floor, and led the way to the second floor past the floral wallpaper, the banister painted in eggshell, the waxed hardwood floors, and the window at the top of the landing. Tommy unlocked the door to the apartment on the left numbered three, reached around the wall to turn on the lights and motioned for Carol to step inside.

"I'll give you the tour," Tommy said, pointing to the small dining room and kitchen entrance. "The kitchen is small but everything works. Over here, the living room. The television is old but still has a good picture. The bedroom has a full size bed, dresser, and a chest of drawers. What do you think?"

"This is beautiful! Do you mean I can live here? For how long?"

"As long as you want, if you keep your part of the deal. Do we have a deal?"

"Yes."

"Shoot." He took out his phone, opened his notes application, and sat on the sofa. Carol sat in the chair next to him.

"Robert runs this game. He seduces rich housewives into telling him things about their husbands' businesses. The women don't always find out he blackmails their husbands behind their backs and the husbands haven't a clue their wives are cheating on them with Robert. The men pay off. Robert dumps the women and moves on."

What kind of information?"

"He doesn't tell me, but the secrets are big enough that no one calls the cops. Then he moves on to the next mark. It's amazing how many times he gets away with it, but he does. It's one of his favorites."

"As far as what he's up to now, all I know is he knew Leah before me. They used to be a team. She got in touch with him to get him to help her. Robert insisted this set up was all business, but I had to get a look at her. I thought he was worth fighting for. That sounds pretty dumb when I hear it out loud."

"Anything else I should know? Does he carry a weapon? Any other partners?"

"Except for Leah, I don't know of anyone else he works with. I know he plans to threaten Leah as leverage if you won't play along. He went to the restaurant last night to make it seem believable he picked up his information on you by overhearing your conversation in case you started to suspect Leah. That was the last time I saw him."

Tommy had been typing notes off and on. He stopped and

waited to see if she had more to say.

She did. "This whole thing sounded messed up. He told me you were in organized crime. I told him in that case it would be too risky if you found out his name. He left the restaurant and said he would meet me at the apartment. When he didn't show, I went looking at your place. You know the rest of the story."

"I doubt it. What else did he say?"

Carol licked her lips. After a few seconds, she continued, "He said they were splitting fifty-fifty. She plans to play along with you for a while, find a reason to break up, and then move somewhere else with money to burn. Is that what you wanted to know? I don't know if I left anything out."

"That's not what I *wanted* to know, but I have what I need," Tommy said, gripping the sofa pillow under him. He brought his emotions under control before speaking. "Will he be looking for you tonight? If he does come back, will he be suspicious that you're gone?"

"I doubt if he'll be back. One thing I want to ask you is if you're with the mob. You seem more like a cop."

Tommy scoffed. "The only thing criminal about me is my temper. No one wants to be played for a fool."

"I'll take your word for it. Whoever you are, no one has ever given me a chance like this, and I won't forget it."

"Let's call us even. You've practically saved my life, at least saved me from making a huge mistake. I've got to go now," Tommy said. He stopped at the door and turned. "There's some food in the refrigerator when you get hungry, and soap and shampoo in the bathroom. I'll be back tomorrow to check on you."

Carol looked at Tommy. "I'm sorry about your girlfriend."

"I'll get over it," he said.

Tommy called his father on the drive home to relay what he had found out, and his subsequent plans. He ended their conversation when he arrived at home a few minutes after four.

Leah called out from the kitchen, but he did not answer her. He stood in the doorway and watched her. Seeing her performing simple domestic chores, he had difficulty reconciling her with the woman Carol had described. His pride resisted the notion that someone he loved and trusted enough to invite into his private world could fool him. He wanted to believe he was too smart. The stinging part of being made a fool of is learning that it says as much about the deceived as about the deceiver.

"You're here," Leah said. "Hungry? I can make something."

"Nothing heavy. I'm changing to go the gym." He knew the one way to keep from beating her within an inch of her life was to do a hard workout. He made a quick change, tucked his cell phone in his sweatpants pocket, and headed to the front door. "I won't be gone long."

He heard her say something, but he ignored the draw to engage. He had to keep focus and control. Venting would come later. He ran down the stairs to the gym on the mezzanine, already sweating, pulse pounding. Confrontation pending. His phone rang when he reached the first weight machine. He stepped over to a quiet corner and answered.

"Yes?"

"Bring the money to the Fore and Aft at six tonight. "There'll be a packed room of people, so don't get any ideas. Wrap the bills in a towel, roll it up tight, and put it in the trash bin in the men's room. Go to the bar. When I see you, I'll know it's done. Don't try to figure out who I am. Got it?"

"Got it." Tommy heard a disconnecting click.

Almost the instant the first call ended, a second call came in. He pressed to accept and spoke, talking in low tones as he made his way back upstairs until he reached his apartment.

He heard Leah still shuffling pots on the stovetop. He looked at the clock. After five. Plenty of time to get to the Fore and Aft without rushing. Better for Leah and for him if he stayed away from her right now. He changed into jeans and t-shirt, and slipped out before Leah knew he came and went.

He recognized Robert from the surveillance video. Tommy studied his character through his mannerisms and clothes, measuring him as a rival more than a blackmailing scumbag. Robert looked down at his watch, and rubbed his face either from nerves or from habitual drug use. Tommy recognized a jittery cockiness about this man, who believed he controlled the game.

The restaurant drew hundreds of office workers on their way home Monday through Friday. The crowd today congregated on the outdoor patio, laughing, drinking, eating finger food. Tommy seated himself inside the small bar area filled with a sprinkling of executives clustered in the corner. Tommy felt Robert's eyes on him when he carried the package to the men's restroom. When Tommy returned to his seat, he ordered a beer, and pretended to be curious about a group of executives. Out of his peripheral view, Tommy watched Robert make his way to the drop, and waited for him to come out.

The sticky air was cooler than last night, but still effective at keeping Tommy damp around his neck. He waited until Robert swaggered out with the package and a self-satisfied grin. Tommy thought Robert's eyes looked glassier than before, but drugs were not the issue for today. His problem was about to be handled in a permanent way. He sat back, took a sip of beer, and made casual eye contact with Robert.

Tommy grinned as Robert went from cockiness, to disbelief, to panic, and at last to rage as the men from the corner surrounded him and took hold of his wiry body.

"What the hell is going on here? Get the fuck off me!"

"Settle down, little man. You're under arrest. You have the right to remain silent." One of the men tossed him into the arms of two uniformed officers who appeared from the dining room. "Don't forget to read him his rights. We wouldn't want this slimy one getting back on the streets on a technicality."

Tommy stayed in his seat, nodded to the men, and watched them file out through the front door no more conspicuous than any other patron. Smiling came easy for the first time since he received the morning call. One down. He expected the next part to go easy and to be more satisfying.

Tommy stepped off the elevator anticipating his next move, taking a sadistic pleasure that Leah had no idea the life she knew today was over. The short drive from the restaurant to home had given him time to get used to the idea of life without her. He had lived an eternity today, as if the universe had pulled him through the eye of the proverbial needle. Exhaustion was setting in, urging him to give into sleep, but he had to hang on for the next hour. Then, a long, healing, restful sleep. He stood in front of his door, inhaled, exhaled, and closed his eyes for focus. Whether by adrenalin or determination, he found a sudden surge of strength and turned the doorknob.

"You look beat," Leah said. She surprised him at the door. "Come in and sit down. I'll make you a drink. You must be hungry too. You left without eating. Want me to warm it for you?"

He studied her. She had assumed that arrogance Robert displayed seconds before his arrest. Would her expressions go through the same transformations in the next couple of minutes?

"So, what've you been doing? You rushed out so fast. A business emergency?"

"You might say that. I watched your boyfriend get arrested at the Fore and Aft."

He smothered a laugh when her face went pale.

"What?"

"You heard me," he said. "It's over. No money. No Robert. No Tommy. You're done."

"Wait. I don't know what he told you, but I had nothing to do with this. Baby, you know I love you. I wouldn't do anything to hurt you."

"Save it," Tommy said. He walked to the door and opened it. "She's ready."

"Who are these guys? Oh, God. You're having me murdered."

"Shut up, you stupid bitch. Can't you see they're cops? Please get her out of here before I lose my control."

"What is this? The cops working with the mob now?"

A female officer took her arm, twisting it behind her, and pulled out the handcuffs. In another strategic movement, the officer rushed her out into the hall, restraining her so she could not turn around.

"Since I paid for everything, I'm donating all of it to Goodwill tomorrow. I'll see you in court," Tommy called out.

He heard her ask the officer, "Can he get rid of my clothes like that?"

If not for the police outside in the hall, he would have slammed the door. Instead, he pushed the door to its jamb as gently as he could, turned the lock, and backed away. He walked into the living room, and sat in a space normally welcoming and comfortable.

His fatigued eyes took in the sterile environment with its pristine furnishings that restored his sense of order, thanks to his housekeeper. Now the room looked lifeless and devoid of the human factor that would create coziness.

Loneliness swept over him. He needed to sleep, but he could not sleep in the bed still fresh with her smell in the bedclothes. He pulled his phone from his pocket and flipped it open. When he had scrolled to the housekeeper's number, he texted her an urgent message to come tomorrow for the whole day. Done.

He grabbed a small duffle bag, stuffed it with sweats, underwear, his DOP kit, and a bottle of water. A hotel appealed to him. Sleep in a fresh bed in an impersonal room.

He checked out of the hotel early the next morning and went grocery shopping at the Kroger's near Carol's new apartment. He had no idea what to buy, so he looked for clean foods, healthy, organic, low fat. By the time he knocked on her door, he needed to make two trips to carry the bags.

"Was it awful?" Carol asked, after Tommy briefed her on the previous night's events.

"It was the hardest thing I've ever had to do."

"I'm sorry."

"Don't be. People get hurt all the time," Tommy said, but he did not mean it. He looked at her as if seeing her for the first time. "You look better today."

"I slept well. Today's the first time in years that I woke up believing things are going to work out for me. As soon as I start working, I'm going to pay you back for all this. You can't imagine how it feels getting an opportunity like this. I won't forget it."

"Funny, when you start building your personal empire, you think of returns on your investments, how you squeeze a little more out by cutting back on this or that. But when I think how little the rent means to me and how much it helps you, it puts ambition in perspective."

"You won't be sorry you helped me. There's just one thing I'd like to know."

"Yeah. What?"

"What do you do for a living? I mean, you're a cop, right?"

"FBI. Organized Crime Unit."

Carol started laughing so hard, she soon had him laughing. "The perfect irony."

OPPORTUNITY KNOCKS

The idea came to her the moment poor Uncle Gerald toppled over trying to reach a wine bottle on the shelf, and cracked his head wide open on the stone hearth.

Tina rushed around the room to retrieve a few incriminating items left behind after a previous visit. Now, Ben's cup sat next to Gerald's tumbler on the table, his glove placed under the table.

As expected, once Ben was arrested he gave her power of attorney to handle his affairs while he was in jail. Keeping her on that strict allowance turned out to be another false economy for a cheapskate.

THE USUAL

Noreen paced around her living room, anxious and hesitant about what to do. Eight o'clock. She should be settled in front of the television, reading, or doing anything else but wondering whether or not to go to the bar.

Six months ago, one of her coworkers had invited her to join them for happy hour drinks. She had been flattered to be included. Working in the bank's computer department, she had little contact with the outgoing marketing and personal service staff. But she always took time to stop for a chat with Lyn, the receptionist, and supposed Lyn was responsible for the invitation. That did not matter to Noreen. She was happy to be included at last.

She and her group joined office workers from other companies in the business district in the small and smoky dimly-lit bar. Overcrowded, poor acoustics, and uncomfortable seating had not exactly compared to the fast-paced, glamorous scene portrayed in beer commercials.

After happy hour ended at six, she stayed on to be a sympathetic ear to a woman she had just met who was determined to pour out the details of her messy divorce to a stranger. By the time Noreen escaped, she looked at the people around her. They were slurring their speech and speaking loudly while others were argumentative or sad. The atmosphere had become stifling and oppressive. She muttered to herself all the way home that she would never go there again.

But, the next day, when her coworkers invited her along again, she went. In retrospect, she might admit that it was exciting. Or, more likely, that she found the passive filling up of her evenings a remedy for her acute loneliness. Noreen stayed behind again, imbedding herself in the late night club atmosphere, and striking up new acquaintances who accepted her no questions asked.

After that, she went every night, often right after work. The regulars gave her the kinship and popularity that work never provided. Even after learning that they did not work or have any visible means of support, a fact her mother would have said was "highly *ir*-regular," she set aside the obvious concerns and embraced their lifestyle.

Why not. I have nothing else to do.

Then he came along. She had seen Bo around before, a tall, dark, smoking hot pool hustler with a lot of time on his hands, and a major player in the bar. Noreen had seen how the other women sought out his attention. And their threatening looks when Bo invited her to sit with him the first time. Had it really taken only a few days before they became inseparable? And a quasi-hostess at his place for after-hours parties? Forget that keeping the late hours with him had made her job at the bank more difficult.

Being a constant around Bo, Noreen saw close up the level of secrecy among he and the other regulars. They kept to themselves, kept their conversations out of earshot of others, even away from her most of the time. Deep down, she suspected their covert nature had criminal undertones—that she should get out before it was too late, but she could not risk losing Bo.

This midsummer evening, moist from an afternoon shower, Noreen could not shrug off her concerns. If they were doing something wrong, would the police think she was involved?

Birds of a feather, and all that? She negotiated with her conscience that she would give this issue more thought soon— but not tonight.

She showered, fixed her hair, and dressed. She flung her tiny purse over her shoulder, and walked the few blocks to the bar. Some idea lurked in the background that made her queasy tonight. But once she pushed through the bar's heavy metallic door and caught sight of Bo, her anxiety turned into anticipation.

He stood at the pool table and looked up with everyone else, as they all did whenever the door opened. Before he took his shot, he gave her a wink.

Noreen smile and joined Bo next to the pool table. She watched him concentrate on his next shot and felt the surge of sexual tension between them. His walk, his moves, his clothes, even the little diamond and gold pinkie ring seemed to have a sexual connotation, but the most erotic was the intensity of his concentration. The look in his eyes when he focused on the ball, estimating the impact one had on the next, and calculating its path to the pocket, had the same intensity he had during sex. His hands, his mouth, his lips were no longer utilitarian, but devices of a powerful sexual instrument.

"Hey, Babe," Bo said, walking toward her after winning the game.

"Hi," she said.

"How's work?"

"It's okay. About the same. Lyn might stop in tonight. You remember, I told you about her?"

"Oh yeah. That'll be nice for you to have a friend from work to talk to. You're too smart for this bunch."

He pulled out his wallet and handed her a fifty. "How about getting me a drink? Get yourself one, too." He flashed a broad toothy smile. "I've got another game up."

Noreen leaned against the bar and motioned for the barmaid's attention. "Hi Aggie, a draft please. And a seven-seven for Bo."

"Sure, kiddo. I'll bring them right over."

"Not going to say hi, little girl?"

Noreen turned. "Sarge, hi. I didn't see you."

"That's what all the pretty girls say to dirty old men."

Noreen grinned. Sarge, a seventy-eight year old, ex-Army career man, somewhat emaciated, was an uncontrollable drunk but a great storyteller. He was her favorite character. Sarge played pool with the young boys who came in with attitude, seldom as good as they thought they were. They bet high, believing the win was a given against an old man, and rarely balked when they found they had been hustled.

"I'll talk to you later, Pops."

She saw Bo racking up the balls for a new game, and Aggie making her way over to the table with their drinks. She hurried back to position herself on a stool to watch him. After a few games and several drinks, she started to get bored, even sleepy from sitting tight too long. The green pool table had even started to look wavy to her. Lyn was not going to show, so she moved to the bar to sit with Sarge, and his daughter, Mel, and her husband, Crank, who sat next to him.

Mel and Crank, a crusty biker couple she estimated were in their thirties, both had the weathered look of a life lived hard. Mel's attractiveness was still apparent in her trim figure despite the leather-like texture of her skin from either smoking or the sun, or both. Crank, nicknamed for his drug of choice, was a burly man whose massive height amplified his powerful physique. Together, the couple made a threatening visual.

This evening, the only one around to challenge Sarge was a starchy blonde who looked like she belonged in a college bar more than a seedy downtown dive. Noreen knew the blonde was out of her league, watching her use the tired tactics of the low-cut shirt that offered a generous view of her cleavage, twisting her long blonde hair around her finger, and walking around the table—distractions that probably worked on younger, inexperienced men, but not here.

She played a decent game, but lost. Noreen suspected she was used to winning and looked angry. Sarge took her money and started back to his seat. Whether she resented losing to someone old or was angry that she felt hustled, Noreen could not decide. The blonde reached out her hand in a gesture to shake hands with Sarge, and then wrapped her arm around him in a big hug.

The next few minutes happened quick. Noreen had drunk over six beers so that the scene appeared before her like a surreal dream. Maybe nightmare better described it. The blonde lifted Sarge's wallet from his back pocket, but her subtle hand movement did not escape Crank's sharp eye.

Noreen thought Crank surprisingly agile for a man his size. He reached the girl before she had time to stuff the wallet in her purse. he grabbed her by the neck, slammed her against the wall, and then battered his clenched fist into her jaw several times. Noreen caught a glimpse of yellow hair trailing downward, chasing her head along the wall while blood gushed from her mouth.

The bar went into an instant uproar. Some of the patrons defended the girl. Some were on Crank's side. Then there were others who did not know why they were fighting, but joined the battle by hitting the next person they saw.

Aggie, called out, "Noreen, help me with the bitch." When Noreen joined her, she said, "Into the men's john."

They both took an arm and dragged the girl across the floor to the back of the bar. Noreen barricaded the door by bracing her back against the outer door and used her legs for leverage against the wall opposite. Violent hits against the door jarred Noreen's body. Aggie, unperturbed, tended to the girl's wounds by holding cold, wet towels on her nose while what sounded like the end of the world continued outside. At some point, she must have called 911 on her cell because she told the semi-conscious girl the paramedics were on their way.

Within five minutes, the crashing, slamming, glass breaking, screaming, and crying died down to sobbing by the unfortunate women caught in the middle. Noreen lowered her legs and released the pressure on the door. She peeked out and saw the police and several paramedics. She waved her arms and screamed, "Over here," and held the door open. After explaining what happened as logically and coherently as she could to an officer, two paramedics carried in a stretcher, and Aggie let them take girl.

Noreen took stock of herself and her appearance, and then went to look for Bo. She could not find him inside or outside the bar. She assumed the regulars who were involved in the brawl had gotten away before the cops arrived. The after effects of the violence left Noreen shaky and sickened, but mostly confused. She needed to be held and comforted. She saw several men she did not recognize, disheveled and wounded, putting chairs back in place, and wiping down tables. Aggie had returned to her post behind the bar, serving drinks and first aid supplies.

How bizarre. They act as though nothing unusual happened.

She found her purse soaking in spilled beer on the floor by her stool. She picked it up cautiously and checked its contents. Lucky only the outside was ruined. After she took another look around, she left the bar and walked to Bo's house. Not there. She thought about going home, but decided to sit on his porch steps and wait for him. But after an hour, she walked home.

The next morning, she still shook from the unaccustomed physical stress. She comforted herself wrapped inside a blanket on the sofa. Worrying about what happened to Bo made her feel worse. She called him. Still no answer. She dozed off until noon, and then watched television the rest of the afternoon. At four o'clock, she called him again.

"Hello," he said in his smooth, low voice.

"Oh, I'm so glad you're okay. What happened to you last night? I waited at your place for an hour before giving up and walking home. I was so worried."

"Whoa, calm down. No big deal. After I got in a few licks, I took off out the back door. I knew the cops were on their way. I don't need that. Where were you?"

"Aggie and I were barricaded in the men's john with the blonde bimbo who started the whole mess."

He laughed. "That's pretty good. Listen, I have some people here right now. I'll see you later at the bar. Okay?" His voice was still light, but stern. "Bye."

Wow, had she just been dismissed? He had not asked how she felt, or how the brawl had affected her. He had not apologized that he abandoned her. Well, she was not in the mood for the bar tonight—if ever. If he wanted to see her, he would have to come to her.

After time to think about, Noreen decided she might have overreacted. She called the bar a few hours later and asked for Bo.

"It's me," she said. "I'm worn out from last night. Can you come over here?"

"Well, not right now. I'll be over later."

Noreen was not sure what was going on with him, but she sensed something impatient in his tone. She knew she tended overdramatize, so she put aside her hurt feelings.

She ate a light dinner, and watched a movie until she fell asleep. By nine, she woke refreshed and wide-awake. *He could be here anytime now.* She put on makeup, combed her hair, and waited. When he had not arrived by eleven, convinced he was not coming, she washed her face and went to bed.

Noreen woke up to the doorbell ringing repeatedly. She checked the time on her clock—three in the morning. She froze, clutching her blanket until the noise stopped. When the phone rang, she reached her hand to the nightstand and pressed the call button.

"Hello."

"What the hell's wrong with you," Bo said. "I thought you wanted me to come over."

"But I meant a lot earlier. I didn't expect you to come at this hour. I thought someone was trying to break in. I never answer the door in the middle of the night without knowing who it is. If you had told me…"

"You embarrassed me in front of my friends."

"*Friends?* You mean you brought people with you? How could you do that without asking me first." Now she was angry.

"I don't need this. If these same people you see at my place aren't welcome here, the hell with you. Dumb b..." His voice trailed off and she heard him disconnect.

What a jerk. He must be on drugs? He had never spoken to her like that before. Maybe she did not know him as well as she thought. She went back to bed, but had trouble sleeping from the gnawing tension in the pit of her stomach.

She went into work early the next morning to catch up after missing the day before. Considering the last forty-eight hours, she felt right enough, but she needed to heal. After work, she settled on a light salad and a movie that started at eight. She drove home and collapsed into bed. She was beginning to feel like her old self again. The old self before the nightly drinking and staying up until daylight.

The rest of the week and throughout the weekend, she worked late to avoid the temptation of going to the bar, and unplugged the phone to avoid Bo's calls. By Monday, after what seemed like an eternity of self-control, she let her defenses down and spent an early evening at home.

The telephone started ringing at seven thirty. She knew she should ignore it, but she answered anyway. "Hello."

"Where've you been?" His sweet and sensual voice was back.

"I needed a break. Anyway, I'm mad about the way you talked to me. I can't believe your attitude."

"Listen," he said. She could hear the honey dripping from his words. "I'd been partying, had some stuff going on, you know. I wasn't myself. Come on. Don't stay mad. Why don't you come on down to the bar. I'll make it up to you. I promise."

Noreen hesitated "Why don't you come over here instead? I'm not in the mood to go out tonight."

"Come to your house? All evening?"

"Yeah, why not?"

He hesitated at first. "Well, okay."

"Just not at three in the morning. Come early, or don't bother."

"I'll be right over."

He arrived twenty minutes later carrying a twelve-pack of beer and a small bouquet of flowers from the convenience store.

"Thank you," Noreen said. "That's sweet of you."

"My way of apologizing."

"Apology accepted. Take out two beers and I'll put the rest in the fridge. You want to find something for us to watch?"

"Sure," he said. He scrolled through the channels until he found a movie. She snuggled in next to him until the movie finished and they ended up in the bedroom.

"Want another beer or something stronger?" Noreen said. She guided him back to the sofa, but she sensed a change in his demeanor. Instead of wanting to cuddle and watch another movie, he leaned forward, dead eyes staring at the television.

"Listen, I've got to meet some guys at the bar. You want to come?" She saw that he avoided looking into her eyes.

"You're leaving?"

"Yeah. Like I said, I've got to meet some guys. You need to get out, anyway."

Noreen stood staring at him. How could he take her to bed and then want to leave just like that? "Can't you meet them tomorrow and stay here tonight?"

"It's only, what, ten o'clock. That's too early to call it a night. Get dressed. I'll see you at the bar."

"I don't think so!" she said.

"Be there." His tone startled her. "You're just mad about the other night, but you'll get over it." He stood up, looked at her, and then grabbed her by the shoulders. He pressed a deep, hard kiss on her that turned cruel when he bit her lip. She tried to pull away from the pain, but he kept his grip tight. He let go suddenly, she stumbled backward, and reached out for something to grab to keep from falling. Her hand found the desk. She touched her lips and thought she felt blood. She looked up at him. An alarming cruelty in his expression terrified her.

"Don't make me come looking for you." He left her standing there. No goodbye. Just walked through the front door and slammed it behind him.

The loud noise jarred her. She tightened her robe around her and sat down on the sofa. Something not so good happened, but she was too stunned to take in its full meaning. She was angry one minute, hurt the next, and then afraid. His kiss had been an assault as much as if he had slapped her. He meant to intimidate her, and it worked.

She mixed a large vodka and orange juice to settle her nerves, and tried to forget what just happened. She went to the bathroom to check her lip—as she suspected she had a small cut. The blood had spilled from her wound, ran down and crusted on her chin. That would be a swollen mess by morning. She applied an antibiotic gel and went back to the sofa to comfort herself under a large quilt.

She shivered. What would he do when she did not show? Her old clock ticked by the seconds, time passing menacingly to the future.

By two, she thought of taking a drive to settle her nerves, but more to avoid the confrontation when he came back. She filled up her tank, stopped in a twenty-four hour drug store for more antibiotic gel, and topped off the trip indulging her need for comfort at a fast food drive-through. Cruising had been therapeutic. She took a tour around the town's perimeter chomping down fries and a cheeseburger. Normality—just the right prescription to take her mind off her predicament.

But when she turned onto her street, she spotted a car in front of her house. She slowed down and pulled over for a safe view. Bo was leaning against a car she had never seen, openly drinking from a can of beer.

Fear seized her, and she thought for a moment how descriptively apt some clichés were, because "seized" is exactly how she felt in her mid-section. She made a quick turn of the steering wheel, turned down a side street, and drove in the opposite direction. So much ran through her mind. She began to cry. Then, rage took over. She stopped at a pay phone next to the Interstate, and dialed 9-1-1."

"I'd like to complain about a suspicious vehicle down the

street from me. There's a couple of men leaning on the car drinking. The address is 1248 Yates Avenue. I don't think the lady that lives there is home and the men look up to no good."

"We've had other reports on this already. Officers are already on their way," the female dispatcher said.

Noreen thanked her and hung up. She made up her mind to stay at the motel by the freeway. She had no intention of driving up while the police were there and have to admit that she was the reason they were there creating a disturbance. She hoped none of the neighbors recognized him from his earlier visit. *Geez, what a disaster.*

The next morning, she went straight to work without going home. When she walked into the office, Lyn took her arm and led her to the stockroom.

"What happened to your lip. Did someone hit you?"

"No, I bit my numb lip while I was eating ice cream sandwiches." *Could that even happen?*

"If you're sure," Lyn said. "Were you home last night?"

"No. I went to a show and ate out," Noreen said, feeling so grateful she had not confided her double life to Lyn. "Why do you ask?"

"I read about this in the paper this morning. I brought it with me to show you," she said, handing it over to Noreen. "Look, it says that the police approached a car loitering in front of *your* house last night because of complaints from the neighbors. When they asked the men for identification, they found out the two men were wanted. *Wanted!* The cops searched the car and found meth, pot, and a case of handguns in the trunk. Both were arrested on the spot, but the big catch was the car's owner, this Bo Mannix character. Apparently, he's a major criminal. I can't imagine why they were released on bail."

"Released on bail," Noreen said in a whisper.

Lyn enjoyed the drama. After pause for effect, she went on. If she noticed the color had drained out of Noreen's face, she did not acknowledge it.

"The other man, Den Carter, told the cops it was all Bo's

stuff and that he had no idea about what he kept in the trunk. Like, I'm sure he didn't know about it, but it *was* all in the trunk and out of sight. This happened around two-thirty, so I guess you weren't home yet."

"No, actually I stayed in a motel. I saw a mouse and freaked out. I left the house about ten," Noreen said. *Is she falling for this?*

"What a shame you missed all the excitement. I hoped to get the juicy details at lunch today. Anyway, the article says the police have had their eye on this guy for a while but haven't been able to get anything on him. He's been the major source of the drugs coming into town, and suspected of supplying guns to the gangs that have migrated from the west. The police said if it hadn't been for this random incident, they might never have caught him. That bar where we used to go for happy hour is his headquarters. Can you believe it? His picture's in the paper. Do you remember ever seeing him there?"

Lyn held the newspaper closer to Noreen's face, but she could not look. She hoped Lyn did not notice her nervousness.

"No, I don't remember seeing him there." God, was she ever glad Lyn had not shown up that night "I don't think I'd want to go there again. I don't know what they were doing in front of my house. Probably a coincidence. They must've chosen my street as a meeting spot because it's quiet. Or they were waiting for one of my neighbors and just happened to park in front of my house. It's creepy, for sure. It makes me want to move."

"I'll say," Lyn said, her eyes still wide and excited. "Here's the article. I've got to get back to work before the dragon lady writes me up." She gave Noreen a fast grin, and left her alone.

All Noreen could think was how scared she was. How could she be so stupid as to be flattered by the attentions of a good looking man she knew nothing about? She had never asked him questions about his past or anything personal. Her foolishness and desperation must have been apparent to everyone, just as it must have been to him. Easy prey. She had no idea how she to get out of this mess. Maybe she really did need to move. A new neighborhood, at least. She tossed the paper into the trash without reading it.

Noreen went straight home after work with the idea to pack a few days' clothing and stay at a motel. She needed to sort things out. Besides, he would be looking for her. She did not want to be in his path right now.

Her street was quiet now, as if nothing had ever disturbed its tranquility. She reached for her mail, unlocked the door, and walked inside. At first, she looked around in case Bo might be waiting for her. She relaxed when everything looked untouched. She let out a deep sigh and walked into the bedroom.

A strong hand grabbed her head from behind and covered her mouth. The other arm grabbed her around the waist making it impossible to move. She knew this was Bo before he spoke.

"You bitch. Do you really think you had any chance of getting away with that stunt last night? If you had done what I told you to do, I wouldn't have had to come here to get you. Do you have any idea what you've done!"

Noreen tried to speak, but the force of his hand pressed so hard on her mouth and nose left her struggling to breathe. Her squirming to break free was useless against his strength. The more she struggled, the tighter he squeezed. She trembled all over from the panic. She knew he was going to kill her.

Then he seemed to loosen his grip on her waist. She thought that he was not really going to hurt her after all, but had just wanted to scare her. She relaxed, but he wrapped both hands around her neck and started to squeeze. She choked, and gasped, unable to draw air, pulling at his hands to free her neck until she started to lose consciousness. She had given in to an inescapable end when she heard a loud explosion and the sound of a bee pass her right ear.

Bo's hands released their grip on her throat, and his body fell against her. Freed, she dropped to the floor to avoid the weight of his body bearing down on her, and started scurrying away on hands and knees. She heard retreating footsteps, and then the back door slammed. But no sound came from behind.

She turned back. Bo was lying face down with a curious hole in the back of his head, his blood pooling beneath him onto her white carpet. That was never going to come out of the carpet, she thought, and wondered if she was going into shock or just crazy to think of cleaning at time like this. She got closer to check if he might still be alive, but she knew he was dead when she saw his glazed open eyes, a haunting picture she would not soon forget.

"If we can't identify the owner of the gun that shot him, I doubt we'll ever identify your rescuer," an officer said. "I'm sure this had nothing to do with protecting you. More likely the shooter had been following him and took the opportunity when his guard was down."

Noreen wondered if this could get any more humiliating.

"You're a lucky lady," he went on. "I hope this teaches you a lesson about associating with professional criminals."

She knew it could get worse when she looked through her window and saw news vans out in front. Men carrying big cameras on their shoulders raced toward her door, or toward neighbors taking in the scene from their yards. All she could think about was what her mother would say, and the reaction of her boss and co-workers when they heard about this. She could see the looks already. She wished he *had* killed her.

THE PROTECTOR

In the darkness of his bedroom that Cord shared with his ten-month old sister, Annaliese, he listened for the sounds he dreaded to hear that seeped through the wall almost every night. He knew he should not hear these unsettling and disturbing sounds, but he was too embarrassed for his mother to tell her. Before Dad moved out, he guessed that he could not hear anything because his room was the furthest away. But, she moved him into the room next to hers.

"You're only nine and I worry about you being so far away at night. We might not hear each other in an emergency."

They did not have an emergency, but she was right—he heard everything that went on in her room.

He tried to be a good boy since his dad moved out, but his mom did not make that easy. At first, she cried all the time, stopping only to yell at him for *anything*. His stomach churned after school as her got nearer to home, wondering what reason she would find to yell at him for something he did or did not do wrong.

As time went on, she got nicer until she changed back into the mother he remembered. He helped her with the kitchen chores and the yard work that he was strong enough or tall enough to handle. That seemed to make her happy. With weeks left before Annaliese came, life had started to feel normal again.

He saw his dad every weekend, and could have told him about the sounds, but he decided against it. If he got his mom into trouble, she would take it out on him. Instead, he talked about his school grades and the track team. He avoided talking about Mom altogether when he saw the sound of her name brought pain to his dad's face. That hurt Cord. He decided to keep his problems at home to himself. He believed, as he had learned in church, that problems had a way of working themselves out if you have faith.

He listened to Annaliese's steady breathing, and smiled at her gentle snoring. He loved his little sister now, but he could not forget that she had created the problems between his parents. They did not think he understood, but he did. He knew that he was his dad's son but she was not his dad's daughter. She was the unwanted visitor that never left. His dad did not want her there, so he had chosen to leave them rather than to be around her. Cord would not forget that leaving Annaliese meant leaving him behind too, but he still loved his dad.

Now that he had time to get used to having her around, he felt sorry for Annaliese. Dad had told Mom that he did not want anything to do with *that baby*. Annaliese would notice when she was grown, like him, that his dad did not want her around. Cord recalled how the kids at school treated that new boy who did not speak much English and spoke with an accent no one could understand. They pretended the boy was not there when he tried to be friends, and never included him. Cord knew they were wrong, but never stood up to them to protect the boy. A lump rose in his chest whenever he thought about the boy's hurt expression and imagined Annaliese feeling the same way.

He stared out the window to study the sky. There had been a full moon that night too when Dad sent him to his room because he wanted to talk to Mom. They never knew that he always left the door open a crack and listened to them, hoping to hear plans for a vacation during his leave from the Marines.

Cord had opened the door and kept alert for their voices. Something different in his dad's tone scared him. He strained to hear. His dad's words confused him, and frightened him.

"Did you think I wouldn't figure it out? Were you going to pass off another man's bastard on me?"

His mom cried and talked at the same time, like he did when he knew he was in trouble. "I made a mistake. I'm sorry. I wish I could take it back, but I can't. Do you expect me to have an abortion?"

"Yes, I do. Do you expect me to look at that child every day? A constant reminder of how you betrayed me? I couldn't begin to try to start over with that bastard in the house."

"Well, I won't do that. It's a mortal sin. I refuse to murder a baby to make your ego feel better."

"Then you go to *its* father for help. And don't think you're going to keep Cord away from me to get even."

"Please. Don't do this," she said, her words came out in gulps.

"You're the one that did *this*, not me. If you know nothing else, know this: I will never forgive you."

All Cord heard after that was the slam of the back door and Mom crying. A sickening ache in the pit of his stomach told him his world had changed forever.

Life did change, but he held onto the memories of the short time between his dad's return from Iraq and the time he moved out. He concentrated hard to keep the last good memories of all of them living together fresh in his mind, even though his parents barely spoke now.

His favorite memories always had to do with his dad— hikes and bike rides in the evenings, road trips on the weekends, visits to the hardware store, or helping him in the garage. Sundays, he had listened to the stories between Dad and his friends about the war while Mom and the other wives served picnics in their back yard. No matter where he went, at school or playing with his friends, Cord felt his Dad's presence inside him—his guardian angel.

When he was still in Iraq, his dad Skyped them when he could. Being able to see him on the computer screen, and talk to him as if he were with them, his dad never seemed far away. Now, his dad lived minutes from their house, but he seemed further away and more disconnected. The only calls now were on Fridays to say he was on his way to pick him up, when his mom just handed him the telephone without comment.

Before Annaliese came, Mom had started giving him all of her attention again. After school, they ate dinner and watched television or played board games, talked about the baby that would join them soon, or what happened at school that day. She cried a lot, but reminded him that she and Dad still loved him and always would, but that she had made a horrible mistake that made it impossible for things to ever be the same again.

Once Annaliese came, she did not have time to be his mother anymore. The baby needed her all the time. He could not count on her. If he asked her to play a game, she told him to learn to take care of himself because his sister needed her. When she was not cooking, cleaning, or taking care of Annaliese, she slept or stared at the television. She was always too tired to listen, except when she heard him opening a cabinet or the refrigerator.

His Dad's nearby apartment was clean, but Cord felt bad that his Dad lived alone with nothing on the walls and nothing in the kitchen that Mom would allow them to eat. He wished he could live there with Dad all the time. He could make it nice for the two of them. He told his Dad that it would be great to spend all their time together like before, but his Dad had looked at him funny and had not said anything. Something from that hesitation told Cord that his dad did not want him around all the time.

His stomach tightened. He knew that his world had drifted even further into the scary darkness where his parents were strangers to each other, but also to him. His security had evaporated. Now he had to be strong and learn how not to be afraid on his own.

He leaned against the wall to listen for the sounds. He looked at Annaliese again. Still sleeping. *What a relief.* The peace in her expression calmed him. Her well-being mattered to him now, and always would ever since he heard their neighbor talking about his family.

Bea, retired and widowed according to his mom, had been drinking tea with a friend on her front porch. He had been practicing his soccer moves around the side, but stopped when he heard his sister's name.

"They call the poor little bastard Annaliese. How pretentious. I have no idea whose last name she has. You know, the husband left her over this. I heard it all from my bedroom window one night. That baby's starting out life with a handicap like that. Imagine it," Bea said.

"What chance do either of those children have being raised by a tramp like that? It's always the children who suffer for their parents' sins," Bea's friend said.

Bea had flushed when she realized Cord heard her from the side yard. She and her friend smiled at him, but hurried inside her house, avoiding his eyes.

He wanted to cry at first, not sure if he were mad or hurt. When he thought about the words later, he decided Bea was right. Annaliese *was* a poor bastard. She was pitiful and illegitimate and she would never know how it felt to be loved as both of his parents had loved him and cared for him when he was smaller. From that moment, he knew that he had to be the man of the house. He was the only person left to protect Annaliese.

Before that happened, he had considered her an alien—an intruder who had destroyed his family. Now, when he said his prayers, he asked God for forgiveness for those mean thoughts and promised he would be a good boy. Mom said he was a good boy when he agreed to let her put the crib in his room until she converted the office into a nursery. He could not imagine how horrible it would be if Annaliese still slept in his mom's room with all those sounds.

When Annaliese turned six months old, Mom had a birthday party for her. He had never heard of the kids on television getting six-month birthday parties, but he guessed it was okay. There was a feeling of relief in the air. Mom seemed better and looked happy like she had before Annaliese was born. Now, she would pay attention to him again. The cake on the table and Annaliese in her high chair, they had started singing "Happy Birthday" when the doorbell rang.

Mom had invited a man named Mike to join the three of them without telling him. Cord wondered how Mom knew him. This stranger kept grabbing her around her waist and trying to kiss her on the neck. She giggled and kept pointing at Cord and backing out of his view. Cord ended up amusing Annaliese when she started to whimper. His mom stayed in the kitchen most of that afternoon, laughing and talking, coming in to check on them occasionally, but never sitting to join him and Annaliese. Back to being isolated and lonely, but also resentful. She could have at least told him she had invited a stranger, and told her so later.

"Listen here," she said. "I don't owe you any explanations. I'm the parent, not you. It's no business of yours who I invite here. I don't want to hear another word.

After that, Mike came over a lot. Cord had looked forward to spending time with his Mom once Annaliese was easier to handle. Instead, she spent that time with Mike. Whenever he told her how he felt, she would say things he thought were dumb.

"This is the last time I'm going to tell you this. I need to find a new husband. We need someone to take care of us. Grown-ups have needs you'll understand when you're older. I want you to start looking at Mike as a new dad."

"I already have a dad."

"You're getting on my nerves. I know you already have a dad, but he's not here, is he? He's not here helping me pay the bills, fixing things around the house, helping me take care of you two kids. Mike wants to do those things for us, so you start treating him with respect." Cord studied her and thought that Annaliese was not the only other person in this house who needed protection.

Cord decided his Dad would be hurt, so he kept Mike out of their conversations when he saw him on the weekends. Not until this last weekend had either of them talked about Mom. When Dad said he was proud of the way he was coping with having a new father, Cord had replied that he already had a father. His Dad corrected himself and said, *stepfather,* and that he wanted to see pictures of him in the wedding.

When his dad realized that Cord had not known, he called his Mom, yelling at her insensitivity.

"I know he's just a kid, but he has feelings, for Christ's sake. You can't shut him out of every decision you're making. I could understand keeping secrets when you decided to go whoring around."

The arguing went on but Cord stopped listening. The shocking news that this man would be there all the time, he lost hope of getting back his mother's attention. This was not the first time he was scared, but now he felt panic for his physical well-being. The idea that Mike would be in their house making decisions about how they would live made him sick. Mike had talked about moving out of state. If he married Mom, they could move them away from his Dad forever.

For the rest of that weekend, his Dad watched movies and played video games with him, hugging him, messing up his hair, or giving him crushing hugs.

"Everything will work out. You'll see. There's no way I would ever let anyone take you away from me."

Cord thought his dad must think he was pitiful, but he did not care. Who could he count on? Who he could trust? Then, he thought of Annaliese. He had to be strong. He had to be around to protect her. He had to find a way to protect them both.

Those sounds were starting again. He put his hands over his ears, but knew they would fall away as soon as he relaxed his arms. He tried a pillow over his left ear but the space under the right ear allowed the sounds in. The sounds his mother made were horrible and frightening. He had no idea how to make it stop. Until now.

At dinner tonight, Mike had reminded Mom that he was leaving at ten thirty and asked if she would make the usual for him.

"Where are you going this time?"

"Taking a load of beef to Springerville. Don't know after that," Mike said, turned and winked. "Haulin' swingin' meat, eh Cord?"

Cord always thought that sounded funny and grinned in spite of his mood, but Mom was not smiling.

"I worry about that drive through Salt River Canyon. All those hairpin turns and steep roads. Isn't there another way to go?"

"Only way is out of the way. I've made that trip a hundred times. I'm a good driver; I don't take chances. I'll be fine."

"If you say so," she said. She gave him a concerned look that Cord found annoying.

"Going to make my lunch again?"

"Sure. I'll get it ready after dinner. The usual?"

"I sure love your cooking, hon. Whatever you want to make for me is fine. My only request is my thermos of coffee."

His mother grinned and touched the top of Mike's hand. Cord trembled with rage. He wanted to make sure he got his thermos, too.

The stainless steel thermos, hot to the touch, gleamed like a beacon in the low-level light from the microwave clock. Beside it, the large plastic Tupperware container holding sandwiches, donuts, cookies, and devilled eggs sat nearby.

Once he heard them go into the bedroom, he sneaked into the kitchen and opened the thermos. With his gloved hands, he poured out a third of the hot coffee and replaced it with Everclear alcohol he had hidden in the cupboard behind the Vodka last week.

Cord remembered his dad talking to Jed at the General Store near the campground. They had been talking about propane, when Jed said that Everclear was great fuel to use for a portable stove, but tasteless and too strong for drinking. Jed had said his cousin had died from drinking it on a dare, choosing not to believe its potency. Dad had agreed it was not a risk worth taking. When Cord found a bottle stuck in with the camping gear last week while looking for his backpack, he knew what he had to do.

Watching Mike gulp down coffee all day gave Cord the idea to put something in the thermos. If Mike got a DUI while driving a company truck, maybe they would put him in jail, he would lose his, and Mom would not marry him. He hoped this would get him out of here and away from his family.

He heard her door open and she called out, "Cord, if you've finished loading the dishwasher, take out the trash. Then, take a bath and get to bed. School tomorrow, you know."

"Okay, Mom," he said.

"What, no argument to play a game? What's gotten into you?"

"Nothing," Cord said.

He hoped this would be the last time he had to hear those awful sounds. The clock blinked in red numbers that it was ten fifteen. He listened to the whispered conversation, the footsteps in the hallway passing his door, the shuffling of suitcase and plastic bags of supplies, and then the front door closing. Moments later, he heard his mom's bare feet walking past his door, sticky with sweat—giving off a faint pulling sound as each foot lifted off the wood floor.

The tractor-trailer roared as the ignition sent currents of life through the sleeping engine. Cord peeked out his window to watch the big machine move from its parking space into the middle of the residential street and turn onto the main road out of his view. He checked on Annaliese, and then got back into bed with a sense of relief. He fell asleep as soon as his head sank into the pillow.

He knew something bad had happened by the look on his mom's face the next morning. She stood over him, her eyes red and puffy.

"You're staying home from school. I need help today. Get the baby up and give her some breakfast."

She started back to her room, but turned around and put her hand on his shoulder. "Cord, sweetheart, I have bad news. Mike lost control of his truck last night and died in the crash. The police said the accident wasn't his fault. He tried to swerve to keep from hitting a car, and his semi overturned and went over the guardrails. I'm sick thinking about his last moments. Please help me get through this, will you? If you take care of Annaliese, that would be a big help to Mommy. Will you do that?"

"Sure, Mom. I'm sorry."

"I guess it's just us again. I thought I could make us a new family, but it wasn't meant to be."

Cord watched her move into her bedroom and shut the door behind her.

Annaliese was half standing, half leaning on the rails of her crib. She smiled and started clapping when she noticed him watching her. He scooped her into his arms and carried her to the kitchen. Then he noticed the familiar, unpleasant odor. He carried her back to the bedroom to change her diaper. She looked up at him, grinning and waving her hands to play. He tapped her nose lightly, and smiled at her.

"We're going to be alright, little sister."

CREEPY JOINT

Ruby Gentry closed the trunk of her Honda Accord and turned to face Ellen Zadora, who stood on the curb with her hands on her hips. Ruby's eyes moved from her best friend to the winter sun. She dreaded the trip to Somerton. Her stepbrother, Clifton Thoms, had insisted she come to him to collect her late father's belongings and keepsakes. This sentimental pilgrimage closed a chapter in her life—a final sad salute to her father's life. This journey also signaled the end of the tenuous relationship she shared with her stepbrother. She grinned. Another symbolic yin-yang dynamic, such as what had marked her life as far back as she could remember--shadows and light, hot and cold, good and evil.

"Are you sure I'm up for a trip like this, Ellen?"

"Ruby, sweetheart, would I steer you wrong? If you run into trouble, you have your cell phone to call nine-one-one. What could be easier?"

Ruby sighed. "I'd rather have hired a messenger service to pick up Dad's things. I don't appreciate this pressure at all."

"This is about getting keepsakes your father wanted you to have—not about issues with your stepbrother." Ellen's blonde curls brushed against her cheek when they escaped from her beret and made her appear to wink. "I know what's on your mind, Ruby, darling."

"Do you?"

"Sure, you're thinking you're too frail to make this trip, but that's not so. Remember what the doctor said?"

"Yeah. Since I'm peri-menopausal, I've started to experience estrogen dominance and progesterone deficiency, a common reason for palpitations in a woman of our *sort of age*. According to the cardiologist, the stress of losing my father has exacerbated the condition. But even after they brought hormones under control, I still have a slight arrhythmia"

"Put those lingering concerns away, little girl. You're taking medication for all that now. Loosen up. Find the fun."

Ruby laughed in spite of herself.

"See, you know it's the truth. Now, get your tail in the car and be on your way. You'll never make it before dark the way you're piddling."

"Yep, I'd better get going," Ruby said. She started to climb into the car, but paused and turned. "You know, Ellen, I appreciate your support these last few months. After my mother's death, I fell into a lonely place and couldn't climb out. Your friendship came at the time I needed a friend the most. That means the world to me."

"God, you're not going to get sentimental riding off into the sunset, are you?"

"I guess not." Ruby pursed her lips in a mock kiss and pulled out of the driveway. She experienced a curious pang of sadness at Ellen's receding figure in the rearview mirror. Ruby brushed it off as another yin-yang moment.

Ruby leaned back in her seat after negotiating a clear spot in the middle lane of I-10, and let the cruise control.do the rest from the Loop 303 to the AZ-85 exit. She popped a butterscotch drop in her mouth, and glanced at the digital clock in the dashboard that read six fifteen. Her peripheral vision caught a farmhouse situated close to the road. She kept her eye on the house, waiting until it began to form a stippled image in the distant landscape.

Without warning, the car engine shut down with a heavy clunk that felt as though something gave way beneath her. Adrenaline surged through her body. Her heart pounded. She steered the car off the pavement to the side of a grassy shoulder. Toxic fumes of burning rubber and oily metal assaulted her nostrils. She wanted to give into the idea of getting sick, but told herself to be strong. She had to find help.

She opened the door, stepped out into the chilly air and looked at her surroundings. The full moon provided hazy glow over the fluffy white bolls in the unharvested cotton fields and the farmhouse beyond. A sensation of complete isolation rippled through her body. Stranded and vulnerable in an unfamiliar place, she started to tremble. She fumbled to touch something solid and reliable.

Her purse lay open on the car seat, and she brightened when her eyes fell on her cell phone. She leaned over and plunged her hand inside her bag to retrieve it. She took it from its holster, and gasped. When she pressed the power button, not even a flicker of light flashed on the small square screen.

"I hate technology! Why the *hell* didn't I switch it on before I left?" Something must have been wrong with the battery. Ruby had seen Ellen plug the cord into the charger when she helped her get ready for the trip. It struck her then that she had not brought the charger. She closed her eyes, and tried not to cry. Rage overtook frustration and she hurled the phone with all her strength. It broke upon impact on the door handle.

Not sure what to do next, she looked behind her and studied the farmhouse she had seen a quarter mile back. She grabbed her purse, and slammed the car door shut. She had a better chance of finding help there than she did waiting for another car to stop.

Tramping on uneven ground at the side of the blacktop slowed down her pace. Sharp rocks bored into the soles of her loafers. She kept glancing behind her for traffic, but she had not seen any vehicles from either direction. She knew from past trips that Highway 85, the state road between Buckeye and Gila Bend, did not get anywhere near the traffic of the

Interstate. Her anxiety created scenarios where she became prey for a rapist or serial killer.

Fear trickled down the back of her neck like an icicle. She shuddered. Only a few days ago, she had watched the reenactment on a forensic program about a man who had kept a woman's body inside a freezer in a moving van on his driveway years before the police caught him. A young woman alone and stranded on a dark roadside had accepted help from a stranger. Her fate had been sealed because her car had failed her in the wrong place at the wrong time.

Her heart thumped against the crucifix resting on her chest as she walked. Her mind alternated between horrific scenarios until she arrived at the dirt driveway in front of the house. She paused to calm her nerves. Her breaths had grown short. She took in deep gulps of air to slow her breathing. She needed to be calm.

Ruby wiped a tear from her cheek and urged her legs to move forward. When she walked onto the covered porch and knocked on the door, she did not see any lights inside. After a few more tries with no answer, she peered in through the eyelets of the lace curtains and called out, "Anyone home?"

Her dread penetrated the silence in a groan. The people who lived here were not in. Now, she had to wait for them to return in this chilly air. She leaned her back against the door, and looked in both directions. An impulse came over her that she justified by circumstance. She turned to face the door, and took the doorknob in her hand to test how far it would turn. To her surprise, the door started to swing inward.

Once she entered the house, tension set her pulse racing. The large living room and its cozy furnishings looked to belong to people in their fifties or sixties, settled, gracious, and not the sort to turn away someone in trouble. On the other hand, he or she could become upset or angry that she had trespassed, violated their space. She frowned, envisioning herself in a small town jail, or shot as an intruder.

"Hello. Is anyone here? My car broke down and I need to use your phone." Hearing the annoying nasal pitch in her voice, she cleared her throat and spoke again. "Don't be afraid. I didn't mean to walk in like this, but I really need help. Hello."

Her legs trembled from her knees to her feet. She wanted to keep moving but her feet seemed glued to the floor when she tried to take a step. Doubt and indecision intensified her anxiety. The harsh shadows cast by the full moon created moving images in her peripheral vision. Minutes ticked by like hours. She inched to the kitchen doorway and slid her hand over the wall on both sides until she found a light switch plate. She flicked the toggle up and down but her effort only produced a clicking sound.

"Somebody didn't pay the light bill," she said. The singsong tone of her voice sounded tinny and artificial. She glimpsed the outline of two lanterns on the kitchen counter by the window, so she moved further into the darkness. Her fingers touched a box of matches beside the lamps, giving her the injection of confidence she needed. She checked the oil in the clear fuel tanks and saw they had ample levels. She turned the sprocket knobs to raise each wick, lit them, and secured the glass chimneys.

She blew out a relieved sigh. With the room now in soft light, she saw an inviting family gathering place. She carried a lamp to the large kitchen table and sat on one of the wooden chairs, and soaked in the comforting atmosphere. She enjoyed the calm after the emotions of the past hour. Outside, the wind kicked up, swirling around the house, gently disturbing something metal. The sounds relaxed her body, making her earlier fears seem childish. She looked for a telephone, assuming a country kitchen like this would have a wall telephone with a long cord for lengthy conversations.

No phone. Disappointed that fantasy did not match reality, she took a lamp and walked into the living room. No telephone there either. Irritated, she figured her last chance to make a call would be upstairs.

A surge of adrenaline set her nerves back on edge as she approached the staircase.

"Steady, girl." Looking up to the black void at the upstairs landing, she kept her right hand on the bannister for stability, advancing upward, one step at a time with the lamp raised in front of her. When she reached the landing, the light from the lamp illuminated a long, narrow corridor with two doors on her left.

Why do the doors have to be closed? I feel like I'm in the *Silent Hill* video game, where those weird nurses are waiting behind the door to slash me to pieces. "Stop it, girl. You're scaring yourself." Her words rang out in a hysterical voice she did not recognize.

She inhaled, and took careful steps to the first door and knocked. No response. She turned the knob and entered the room. At first, the darkness beyond the lamp's light cast a tomblike feel to the small space. Once her eyes adjusted, her lamp cast a weak glow around the room that allowed her to focus on the furnishings. A bed centered on the left wall, a dresser on the right, and a short chest of drawers next to her by the door created a spare, homey retreat. She checked the surfaces of the dresser and chest for a telephone, but did not find one. She had started back to the door, but stopped suddenly when a vague form came into her peripheral view.

The form of a person lying flat across the bed that she had first mistaken for pillows was visible in the dim light. How could even a sick person have slept through her noise? She moved closer, rehearsing an explanation for her presence in the house. She raised the lamp above the bed to get a look. A man's unblinking eyes stared up at the ceiling.

The urge to escape overrode her first instinct to help him. Fear shot through every nerve, beating her body raw from her racing heart to her trembling thighs. She backed out of the room into the hallway, fell against the wall, and grabbed her chest. The pulsing in her neck ran down to her arms. She steadied herself ready to run toward the stairs when she heard a squeaking noise coming from the second room.

"Oh, no," she whispered. The incredulity of the situation, not unlike those surrealistic slasher movies she hated, made her want to giggle out hysterics. She froze with indecision between flight and curiosity. She strained her ears to work out the sound. The closer she moved toward the second door, the harder her chest pounded. Beads of sweat ran down her forehead and into her eyes. Her shaking hands created a jittery light across the walls. Fearful of total darkness, she glanced at the kerosene level.

She took a second in front of the door to build her courage. She turned the doorknob and opened the door just wide enough to step over the threshold. She leaned forward, held up her light, and blinked to focus. Her mind took several moments to process. A figure hung by its neck from the light fixture, swaying from side to side like a pendulum. When the body rotated a quarter turn, her light fell on the contorted face. The eyes bulged out and gaped at her. The purple lips drooped down. The swollen tongue lay on the corner of the mouth.

Ruby's heart began to race, her breathing quickened, and her chest tightened. Her hands grew sweaty. Every muscle of her body shuddered. Ruby reached blindly behind her for the door handle, still keeping a firm grip on the lamp. Danger oozed from the very walls of the house. She lurched forward and staggered down the hall toward the stairs. She glanced behind her, lost her footing, and stumbled on a loose piece of carpet. Off balance and out of control, gravity pulled her backward down the stairs. The hard walls of the narrow stairwell and the steps slammed her as she plummeted to the bottom, groaning and cursing with every blow.

"Crap," she said, patting herself all over and shifting onto her behind. Amazed at finding no broken bones, she opened her eyes to orient herself. The lamp had flown from her hand and now lay in jagged pieces around her. The odor of spilled kerosene stung her nostrils, but, thank God, there were no flames. She got up with care, and shuffled to the kitchen for the other lamp. She squatted to look in the cabinet underneath the kitchen sink for more kerosene. A noise from behind startled her. She jerked around. A tall, bulky man hovered across the room gripping a knife as long as his forearm.

Her chest tightened and her breathing quickened. She felt

around for a weapon but only found plastic containers and spray cans in the cabinet. She grabbed an aerosol can and aimed, thankful for the toxic odor of oven cleaner emanating from the can.

The dark shadow flew across the room at her in a seamless movement, the knife raised in one hand while the other dangled at his side. She freed herself from the paralyzing fear long enough to rise up to meet him. She closed her eyes and pressed the nozzle.

He stopped but kept the knife raised. The pause gave her an opportunity, so she ran toward the living room. Before she reached the front door, another man rushed at her in a motion so swift and effortless he might be floating. Trapped, nowhere else to run, she turned and fled back upstairs. The broken lantern glass crunched under her loafers, and she almost slipped on the spilled kerosene.

When she reached the first bedroom door, the strain of fear and physical exertion had brought her close to collapse. She set the lamp on its surface and struggled to scoot the chest of drawers against the door. Little idea of what to do next, she leaned against the wall, closed her eyes and took time to catch her breath. A sudden chest pain surprised her. She grabbed her chest and squeezed her eyes to avoid looking at the corpse on the bed.

Alone, without cell service or a landline, secluded miles from anyone, the likelihood she would survive did not look promising. She opened her eyes and forced them to move toward the dead man. The glow of the lamp dimmed and started to flicker out. Squinting through the darkness, she became aware of something blocking her vision. The man stood directly in front of her, staring, his dead eyes glazed over and unfocussed.

She shrieked. "Oh, God. Somebody help me!" She grabbed at her chest to ease the needle-like pains prickling her. A deafening buzz sounded in her ears. Her vision dissolved into a blanket of red as she gave into the darkness around her. She felt herself falling against the chest and slipping to the floor.

After several minutes of silence, Ellen slid open the pocket door to the adjoining room. She walked over to where Rudy remained motionless. She looked down, and gave a half laugh as she pulled on her gloves, snugging them to her fingertips. She turned around and reached up to loosen the wire that controlled the mannequin. The Halloween prop dropped to the floor with a thud. She picked it up and carried it with her as she scurried back to the second bedroom. She took down the hanging mannequin and dragged both downstairs.

She restored the power at the fuse box outside the back door and watched the kitchen light up. She went to work taking down a mannequin from the kitchen, and another in the living room, and then removed the wires strung along the ceiling perimeters. She pulled out a thermos hidden on a back shelf in the pantry, and began to pour out a rich, creamy hot cocoa. She took a few swallows, and carried a mug with her back upstairs.

She looked down at Ruby. Dead, all right, but touching a corpse was not her style. Between sips, she took out a cell phone and pressed a speed dial number.

"Hey, Cliff. It's me. I'm calling from Ruby's phone. Lucky for me we have the same model phone. Mine's broken to pieces in her car. She must've busted it when she couldn't use it. When I'm done here, I'll put this one in her purse. Before you ask, I've already taken the pieces of my phone out of her car. Make sure to tell the police she called you."

"I won't forget. Quit nagging," Cliff said. Ellen took another sip and started to pace in nervous excitement.

"You won't believe how well it worked. That kill-switch to the gas tank shut down like you said it would."

"Did you ever doubt me? Where's she now?"

"She's on the floor at my feet dead as Moses. I told you a good scare would kill her. I'm surprised she lasted so long. She must've really been scared out of her mind, because she didn't hear me pull around back. I guess by that time, she had enough to worry about with the fake dead bodies all over the place. I almost felt sorry for her."

"Too late for second thoughts. Maybe I'm the one that should be nagging you about the details. Don't tell me you've gotten sentimental?"

"Of course, I'm not sorry. I'm not built for sympathy. I'm putting everything back to normal here in a minute. When they find her, they'll think she stopped here to get help and the stress of the situation gave her a heart attack. Death by natural causes. That's *kind of* what did happen."

"Well, don't get too sure of yourself. This *is* murder whatever way you look at it. Stay cool. Don't get so full of yourself that you make a stupid mistake."

"Hey, I helped you concoct this plot. Don't worry about me. Okay, I have a couple more things to do and then I'm going back to Phoenix. You call the police tomorrow to report that your poor ailing stepsister never arrived. They'll call me once they find her purse—I'm listed as her contact person. When they do, I'll have the perfect reason to drive over to console you. Let's not talk again until then, okay? Cops can trace everything these days. You love me, don't you?"

"Sure," Cliff said.

Ellen hummed when she disconnected the call, and set down the phone. She went back to the second bedroom to make sure she had not overlooked anything that could incriminate her. She went back into the first bedroom, and closed the pocket door behind her. She stepped over Ruby's body by the door and started struggling to shove the chest back into place when she sensed a movement below her.

Hands grasped her ankles and yanked her feet from under her before she had time to react. She panicked, her arms flailing to grab onto something tangible. Her body moved backward in slow motion. Within the fraction of time she had to react, her head cracked against the pointed finial of the footboard.

The sound of wood penetrating bone and brain matter made it obvious to Ruby that Ellen had not survived. She kept an eye on the prostrate woman—just in case. She took her phone from the dresser where Ellen had left it, and used the edge of her blouse to scroll for the last number dialed.

"That slimy sack of shit," Ruby said. She sat down on the bed, resisting the urge to follow the blood pooling under Ellen's startled face. Her outrage at the deception overwhelmed her. The irony was that Ellen was the one person she would have called for help once she found a phone. She sat motionless, thinking about what to do next.

Ruby doubted the police would believe her story. It sounded too fantastic even to her. She had no concrete proof of self-defense. No evidence supporting her claim that Ellen and Clifton set her up. No one to corroborate that they planned for *her* to be the one found dead in an empty house. She would be lucky if the cops *only* charged her with manslaughter. She forced the emotion out of her reasoning so she could think of a plan. When it came to her, she smiled at the ironic justice.

Ruby retraced her steps around the house. She took a kitchen towel with her to smudge everything she had touched. A wiped-down house with absolutely no prints would be suspicious—smears made more sense. The kerosene lamp, shattered and broken in the kitchen and stairwell, most likely had big enough pieces for prints, so she scooped them into the towel, tousled them around to smudge the prints, and let them fall to the floor. In the kitchen, she picked up the aerosol can she had used, gave it a quick rinse under the tap before wiping it down, and replaced it in the cabinet under the sink. Now, she had to make a decision about her car. Ellen had put the mannequins in her own car. They would be easy to dump somewhere on her way home.

Ruby took Ellen's car key off its ring, and replaced it with her own. Ellen had not bothered with luggage, only a handbag. After pulling the car to the side of the house for easy access to the road but still out of sight, she went back inside, for the one last thing she had to do before she cleared out. She went upstairs to the second bedroom, and picked up the phone. She typed a text message: COME QUICK NEED HELP, pressed send, and set it on the chest.

Ruby welcomed the darkness now. She left the house, careful to wipe the front doorknob when she closed the door. She drove Ellen's car beside her own where she retrieved her remaining personal items, and headed back to Phoenix. She had to do this right: call from a public phone instead of a cell phone and be precise about the timing.

She pulled into the first truck stop she saw and spotted a weathered pay phone. She pulled over, grabbed change from her wallet, and went to make a call.

"Nine-one-one, what is your emergency," the operator said.

"I passed a house where I saw two people fighting. I think they were a man and woman. I didn't see a lot but it looked serious. I got a good look at them struggling because all the lights were on. Maybe someone could check to make sure everyone's okay. It's a white farmhouse on eighty-five, east side of the road, about halfway between Gila Bend and Buckeye around the Cotton Center exit. There's a Honda parked a ways down from the house."

"Okay, Ma'am. What—"

Ruby disconnected before the operator had a chance to finish her question. For good measure, she smeared the numbers on the telephone keypad, and drove back to Phoenix.

Ruby waited for the call she knew would come from the Maricopa County Sheriff's Office once they found her abandoned car. When the deputy introduced himself, she took a deep breath, and then waited until she was steady enough to give her rehearsed speech.

"Ellen is a good friend who insisted I take her car for my trip to Somerton. My car isn't always reliable, so we switched. I experienced some palpitations last night and decided to leave later today instead."

"You have a health condition?"

"My heart, but it's a combination of things. Bottom line is I have to take it easy. Not get stressed. To be honest, I started to have anxiety about the idea of travelling."

"Why were you going to Somerton?"

"My stepbrother, Clifton, lives there. After my father died, he cleared out his house. He has my Dad's stuff ready for me to pick up."

"What's your stepbrother's full name?"

"Clifton Thoms."

After a hesitation, the officer continued, "Does he know your friend, Ellen?"

"I don't know how he possibly could. I only met Ellen this past year, and while I've talked about my stepbrother, they never met."

"I need to inform you that your car is part of an ongoing investigation and is in the Maricopa County Sheriff's impound lot."

"What! An investigation? For what?"

"I'm sorry, ma'am. I can't give out that information."

"But what about my car? How long do you need it?"

"Someone will be in touch, ma'am. Thank you for your information."

Once the call disconnected, Ruby said, "Serves you right." She shook her head wondering why Clifton and Ellen hated her enough to try to kill her.

Then the phone rang again. Her caller ID flashed Hal Lakewood. *Why's my Dad's estate attorney calling me?*

"Ruby, it's Hal. I read about Clifton's arrest. Grim business. I had no idea he rented that house. Doesn't look good for him."

"No it doesn't," Ruby said, hoping she hid her self-satisfied smugness well enough. "What can I do for you, Hal?"

"I thought under the circumstances that you should withdraw your power of attorney."

"My what? I haven't given anyone a power of attorney."

"I have one signed and notarized by you giving Clifton authority in all matters relating to the distribution of the proceeds from your father's life insurance policy that went into the trust. He said we were not to bother you. The least disturbance could be fatal with your heart troubles."

"What? I don't understand any of this. What life insurance policy?"

"The $250,000 life insurance policy your father took out about ten years ago making you his sole beneficiary. We sent you letters and received no response. Then Clifton came in with the POA saying you wanted him to represent your interests."

Ruby conjured images of Ellen from the past year—befriending her at the crucial moment coached by Clifton about her illnesses and their shared family history. When Ruby returned from the hospital, distraught about her own health and her father's terminal diagnosis, she had welcomed Ellen's help from paying her bills, checking her incoming mail, to screening calls. She had considered Ellen as selfless friend. Now, she saw that friendship for what it really was—a setup by Cliff, who knew about the policy and how little time her dad had left.

Ruby stifled her first impulse to tell the world—expose Clifton and Ellen for the plans they concocted to see her dead. That's when the reality of her situation hit her.

If she accused Clifton of masterminding this plot, the police might start to listen to his argument that she set him up for Ellen's murder out of revenge. She doubted he would admit to the police that he and Ellen had tried to murder *her*. But if she publicly accused him of this fraud, she would give plausibility to his claims that she had a motive to kill Ellen.

Ruby cleared her throat. "You know, I'd forgotten about that. I *was* sick last year and on many medications. I remember now that Ellen helped me organize those documents to send to Clifton."

"You had me worried."

"Sorry," she said. "Yes I *do* want to rescind that Power of Attorney immediately."

SPIKED HEELS

Monsoon rains ran down Rikki's face and into her eyes as she ran from the house to her car. Her high heels splashed warm puddles of mud on her ankles each time her foot landed on the flooding desert landscape. An awkward shift in her balance threw her out of control when her left spike lodged itself in a crack of flagstone. The force of the momentum slammed her downward. Even the instinctive use of her hands to break her fall had not prevented the impact to her wrists and palms. Or the damage to her face.

Her cheek met the coarse surface and she tasted a bitterness of concrete, probably mixed with her own blood and skin. Mascara melted and ran into her eyes. The pebbled sidewalk scraped her cheek with every intake of breath. The heavy rain acted like a cleansing agent, flushing her eyes, washing away make-up and burning her wounded skin. Once she made the decision to lift herself, she found that action not so simple. Not only her wrists, but also her ankle resisted when she pushed her body to a kneeling position and stood.

She did not need to look to know that her face and hair were not the only cosmetic fatalities. In addition to the ruined water-stained silk dress, her sore ankle resting in the broken shoe told her the black spiked heels were history as well. Her flailing arms had flung the matching clutch ten feet away. It lodged precariously in a Pyracantha bush, visible by the patent leather shining in the moonlight. She consoled herself that its sturdy latch had kept her wallet and make-up bag safe and dry. She removed her shoes and began to hop toward her purse.

She had not seen her keys after the initial cursory glance, and so looked skyward in thanks when she spotted them in a muddy puddle beside the bush. She grabbed her purse from between the thorny branches. Icy water from the wet grass mixed with gritty dirt oozed through her toes. She forced herself not to squeal.

The constant rain that had permeated her clothing now streamed around her curves and down the sides of her legs. Shivering, she supported her wounded ankle as she hopped, triumphant once she reached the sanctuary of her car and shelter from the rain.

Inside the car, she shifted her sore leg and turned on the heater. Cold air burst through the vents and onto her face and chest. The stabbing assault on her injuries brought out a helpless feeling she had not experienced since her childhood. The dampness and cold alone would be enough to give her pneumonia by morning. Unsure if getting soaked from head to toe was how someone got pneumonia, she reached to the backseat for the worn-out fleece jacket she wore during her pre-dawn walks. She had put it in the car because they were supposed to go hiking tomorrow, something that would not happen now. She wrapped herself into the comforting softness of the jacket as faint signs of heat blew out of the vents. Within minutes, the car was almost too hot but that worked well for drying out her clothes and warming up her goose-fleshed skin.

She put the car into gear and pulled away from the curb, taking one last look behind her. With windshield wipers slapping at high speed, she moved into traffic to blend in with other anonymous vehicles making their way through the heavy downpour and erratic winds. Reliving the argument that had instigated the evening's disastrous sequence of events brought back the extreme emotions. The rain pounded down like sympathy as if in response to her tears. Embracing all that was missing or disrupted in the world as a queue for introspection and self-blame, if nothing else, she had self-pity down to an art.

The traffic temporarily diverted her attention from the evening events—her concentration focused on the cars accompanying her on the road and the rain's effect on the pavement. She drove west on Lincoln Drive under the forty-five miles-per-hour speed limit that felt more like sixty-five in the rain. The muted views of elegant homes, lush landscapes, and subtle Malibu lights strategically placed along driveways soothed her. Why she had formed an emotional alliance with a neighborhood she had never lived in drew her into an introspection she preferred not to examine. Maybe its sense of order and identity satisfied her need for structure and place. By the time she neared the interstate, the relentless rhythms of rain and automobile had calmed her. She took a deep breath, and turned north onto the Black Canyon Highway.

By the time she saw the signs for Anthem, the rain had stopped. She pulled into the nearest gas station, and grabbed her wallet before stepping out into the desert night. Above her, the end of the storm clouds had moved and exposed the sky. She took a moment to appreciate the full moon surrounded by black sky dotted with bright pinheads of light. Closing her eyes, he inhaled deeply noting that, unlike people, the desert revived after strong rains. Dusty sidewalks, washed free of subtle layers of sediment, glistened in the glow of streetlights. The purple sage and orange lantana had sharper contrast against the decorative river rock around them. An astringent for the environment that she wished worked the same on her.

She rethought going inside to buy food. Instead, she paid for her gas at the pump and drove to the nearest McDonald's for hot coffee, fries, and a Big Mac. Whether or not it was the healthiest, this comfort food served her best for convenience and cost. She pulled into a parking space to eat, and rummaged through her glove box for wet wipes. Her injured cheek still bled, and had gone beyond stinging to a deep ache. Flashbacks of childhood scraped knees that happened frequently, she knew the wound should be sterilized. The last thing she needed were long term bruises and scabs that made her look like she had been fighting or had fallen down drunk, or both. When she pulled down the make-up mirror on the visor, she realized that her worries were irrelevant. A few dabs of antibacterial would not heal this mess overnight. Between bites, she patted her wounds with the antibacterial cloths. Her ankle and wrists would just have to throb until she found a place to stay.

"What I should be doing is going to an emergency room," she said, but she knew that would be a mistake. She finished the last bits of food, bagged the used wipes with the food containers, and tossed them in a nearby trashcan. When she returned to her car, she got in the back and changed into the sweat pants, hoodie, and flip-flops. She placed her soiled and damaged clothes in a plastic bag, and took a deep breath. "I'll buy what I need later. Thank God for credit cards."

Driving into the desert away from the glow of streetlights, she relaxed and settled down. Intermittent emotional rushes forced her to pull over to dab off the acidic tears running down her facial wounds. Within an hour, she saw the exit for AZ-179 to Sedona, and drove a few miles until she saw the Wildflower Inn.

Trying her best to look respectable, she combed her hair and went into the reception office. The night desk attendant appeared skeptical as she approached the front desk.

"Honestly," she said, "I know I look horrible but I fell off my shoes in the rain."

"Uh-huh," he said. She thought he also looked frightened.

"Please, I just need a room for the night. I haven't just robbed a bank. I had an embarrassing accident and I would like to get a shower and a good night's sleep. Is there somewhere I can get a first aid kit and maybe an Ace bandage for my ankle? I'm pretty banged up."

"We have a gift shop that has first aid items. You can try there.

After the preliminaries, she headed to her room. When she looked back, the desk clerk had turned away from her and appeared to be making a surreptitious telephone call. Stay calm, she thought.

Inside the room away from everyone and feeling protected, as temporary as the sense of security might be, she went directly into the bathroom to shower and wash out her underwear. Not long afterward, clean and dry again, she snuggled in the luxurious bathrobe and allowed herself the painful rerun of that last argument with Mike. She applied antibiotic cream to her face, and winced at the irritation of raw flesh. The analogy was not lost on her how synonymous this physical pain compared to the emotional pain he had inflicted by his verbal lashing.

"So stupid of me to engage. He meant to antagonize me to the point I would leave," she said. Out of the hurt from his words, she used more force than needed when she tightened the Ace bandage over a purple swollen ankle and gave out a moan.

Reliving the argument, she felt her neck heat up from the humiliating words he had spouted at her, "Marry you! I don't remember asking you to marry me. What's wrong with the way things are?"

"Our relationship is tentative. There's no future, no planning. You can't expect me to wait around in the hopes you'll marry me someday. As it is now, I have fewer rights than a tenant. You could toss me out onto the streets at your whim."

"So, you want a lease?"

"No, legitimacy. If you really want to spend the rest of your life with me, then what's the problem? What are you waiting for? Or, am I just convenient until someone better comes along?"

"You bitches are all alike. Anyway to get a hand in a man's wallet."

"That's not fair. Money's not what this is about and you know it. You're saying that to be cruel."

"Then what is this all about? You want me to make an honest woman out of you? Do you believe my parents will look at you as any less of a whore if we're married?"

"You prick. Are you telling me that's what your parents think of me after all I've done for them?"

"And just what have you done for them? It's not like any of the things you've bought them haven't been paid for by me."

"You're the cruelest bastard I've ever known," she said. Despite trying to keep in control, tears began welling up against her will.

"Oh, here come the waterworks. I'm not falling for it. I've spent plenty of money on you since we've been together. When you had your own place, didn't I pay for window repairs, a new air-conditioning unit, and forgave the loan on your car when you lost your job? If anyone owes anybody, it's you. You're not in a position to be making demands on me."

"I didn't ask you for any of those things. You kept volunteering to help me, always telling me not to worry about it. I had no idea you were keeping score."

"I wasn't keeping score, but I didn't forget either."

"What about all that I do around this house now?"

"You live here. The least you can do is to take care of the property. There are no free rides in life, baby. You want to live here, you have to work for it, and that includes in the bedroom."

Remembering how she shook hearing him speak the most horrible words anyone ever said to her, she felt sick all over again. Added to the physical pain, her head started spinning. She found several packets of acetaminophen in the first-aid kit, emptied two packets in her mouth and swallowed. The foremost question in her mind before she fell asleep was how she was going to get her belongings out of Mike's house.

After a heavy sleep, she made her way to the clubroom for the complementary continental breakfast, trying to recall which continent was to blame for the sparse selection. Refreshed and on the mend, she checked out and headed back to the main road until she noticed a boutique close to the Wildflower. She purchased a black velour hoodie with matching pants, new underwear, and a good pair of walking shoes. Her silk dress from the day before, water-stained and ripped in places lay in the bottom of the trashcan in the hotel bathroom, symbolic of more than the disposal of ruined garments—the ceremonious tossing away of that life.

The pain still made her eyes water as each frown brought on by the anxiety of retrieving her things from Mike's managed to disarrange the scabbing process on her injured face.

"Suck it up, girl," she said. She checked her reflection in the rear view mirror, and closed her eyes a moment before turning the key in the ignition. When she opened them again, she looked behind her to see a police car pull up to block her exit.

"What the devil?" she said. Two officers exited their vehicle and walked toward her.

"Can we see some identification, ma'am," the first officer said. His stiff stocky build and thick hands gave him the look of a superhuman folk hero, while his partner, a pared down version with intimidating eyes stood behind him.

The first officer examined her driver's license, made quick eye contact with his partner, and looked into her car. "What happened to your face?"

"I fell," Rikki said. Her heart pounded, blood rushed to her face stimulating her wounds.

"Do you know you're wanted for questioning about an incident that happened last night in Phoenix?"

"No, I didn't. What incident?" Rikki said. Full panic set in and she had to resist the urge to run.

"Please step out of the car, ma'am."

"This is not happening. Oh my God," she said, crying as she struggled to get out of the car. She lifted her feet out of the car and onto the pavement. She took care with her wrists. She saw both officers observing her bandaged ankle and wrists.

Both officers looked at each other. "I think we had better get you to the hospital to be looked at, ma'am," the second officer said. His intense expression had softened.

"Maybe I should. I didn't think I was that bad last night. I was somewhat upset at the time. What are your names, anyway?"

The first officer said, "Brown and he's Jordan. Do you want our shield numbers too?"

"No, I just wanted to know what to call you. Am I being arrested? I guess I'll never get my stuff back now," Rikki said.

"You're not being arrested. You're a person of interest who might be a witness to a crime. From the looks of you, you might be a victim, too. The Phoenix detectives are anxious to interview you. We'll inform them we have taken you to the hospital, but consider yourself in custody until this is figured out."

Later, she tried to remember the sequence of events at the emergency room, but the memory came in brief glimpses like scenes in a passing car. To her distress, the attending physician told her she had several micro breaks in the tiny bones of her feet, one sprained wrist, and a broken finger on the opposite hand, not to mention the damage to her face that would require skin grafting surgery. Life as she knew it was over, she thought when she stared into the eyes of two Phoenix detectives, neither of whom she found attractive. The Vicodin the doctor had prescribed for the pain was taking the edge off her injuries, but also causing some aggression.

"What's this all about? I can't believe that jerk called the police on me. He's got a nerve, is all I can say."

"We just want to know what happened last night. I take it you two had a fight?" the tall, slender, grey-haired officer said. Rikki thought he was playing the paternal type to gain her confidence.

"Yes, we had an argument. He said horrible things to me. I just wanted to get away."

"At what point did he start to hit you?"

"What?" Rikki said, startled by the understanding that they thought Mike beat up on her.

"It's obvious you took a beating. It's a crime, you know. There's no need to protect him. The smart thing would have been to call the police when it happened instead of leaving town, but go on."

Her mind raced. She strained to imagine how someone would get her injuries.

"I…I fell down when he hit me," she said in a whisper, hearing her voice shake, terrified they would catch her in the lie. She saw in their sympathetic expressions that they took her manner to be her fear of Mike.

"How did you get away?"

"I…I think I threw something at him, but I was so scared I just ran as fast as I could to the kitchen for my purse and keys."

"Did he follow you?"

Taking a minute to imagine the scenario, she said, "Maybe he didn't. I felt like if I didn't run as fast as I could, he would catch me. I assumed he followed me but he didn't catch me because I was faster. Is he pressing charges against me?"

"No. I'm afraid I have some bad news for you," the detective said, looking into her eyes. "He was found dead this morning by his mother."

She knew he wanted to gauge her reaction when he revealed that fact, which meant this had to be the performance of a lifetime. Relaxing her face from all expression, she did not have to act when she said, "Oh my God. Are you saying I murdered him?"

"To be honest, that was the idea we got from his mother. But after seeing your injuries, it's obvious this was a case of self-defense. It's not up to us, but we'll have pictures taken of your injuries, get statements from the medical staff here, and take them with us back to Phoenix. You'll have to stay available for questioning. Since you've been admitted to this hospital, if you're released in the next few days, call us with your whereabouts."

"I don't have any place to go," Rikki said, genuinely weepy from her emotions. "Mike's mother hated me before. Now, she'll have more reason to be against me. How do I get my stuff back?"

"Here's my card. Call me when you're ready. I'll give her a call to not disturb anything in the house that belongs to you. I can't guarantee she won't. I'll help if I can."

He set his card on her table, and reached over with a supportive tap on her forearm, then left with his partner following close behind.

She closed her eyes and let her head sink down into the softness of pillows supporting her. She took several deep breaths, as if she had not been able to before. Her body relaxed into the bed and she gave way to the pain medications.

With the last twenty-four hours behind her, she thought how fortuitous that she wore those spiked heels. If not for those shoes, and if not for the accident they caused, she would not have had a reasonable defense. She would have been sitting in a jail cell right now. If not for those shoes, everyone would know self-defense was not the case. They would know that she meant to kill Mike when she threw that cast iron statue at his head with all her strength. They would understand the pleasure she experienced when she watched his stunned face as he slumped to the floor.

She sank deeper into her pillow and fell into a restful, healing sleep.

THE NIGHT OUT

Brenda assessed her middle-aged frame from behind in the full-length mirror. "It's a crime and a *damn* shame," she said, watching her face as she formed the words.

"What are you talking about?"

Brenda sneered at her sister, Bernice, passing by her open bedroom door. "We haven't shared a room since we were teenagers, but I still can't get any privacy."

"If you didn't talk to yourself every time you got ready to go out, you'd have privacy. So what's the problem this time?"

"I'm talking about aging and my ass, if you must know. Look at it. It's getting wider and lower every year. There should be a law against it."

Bernice laughed. "I don't think I've ever known anyone as preoccupied with her rear end as you. Who cares anyway?"

"That's the trouble," Brenda said. "Nobody cares about my ass. Nobody cares about me."

"Oh, here we go again," Bernice said.

"Anyway, I have a date tonight. Maybe he'll have an interest in my ass."

"You *are* a vulgar girl."

"Maybe I am, but at least I'm out there looking. Now that Mom and Pop are gone, you should be too. We don't have to take care of them anymore. The house is up for sale. We're free, and we're going to have plenty of money. Why not live a little?" Brenda leaned into the mirror to apply her lipstick and caught Bernice behind her rolling her eyes.

"I'm not interested in going out like you do. *And* for your information, I meet plenty of nice gentlemen at church. We have a chance to get to know each other to find out if we're compatible. How can you take any of the men you meet seriously when the only thing you have in common is that you both have a drinking problem? That's quite the foundation for a lasting relationship."

Brenda turned around and stepped toward Bernice until their noses almost touched. "I really hate you. I can't wait until this house sells and I can get a place by myself."

"Truth hurts, I guess."

"Don't you have a church choir to join somewhere?" Brenda laughed.

"I guess you find yourself amusing, but you're just a bore." Bernice tilted her head high, grunted, and continued down the hallway.

"Fuddy-duddy," Brenda said. She dismissed Bernice and turned her thoughts back to her reflection. She relaxed her face into a soft smile, adjusted her bra strap, and grabbed her purse. On the walk down the short hall to the living room, she surveyed the house as a stranger might and decided the floral wallpaper her mother put up twenty years ago had to come down. She would think about that later, and by the time she reached the front hall, her thoughts had moved on to her date this evening.

She checked the time. Six fifteen. It would take fifteen minutes to drive to the restaurant. She could be on time and look desperate, or she could arrive a few minutes late and put on a casual attitude. She spotted the "Buddy Book" and took up the pen hanging to it by string. Since they were teenagers, their parents had insisted they leave details about their dates in a notebook by the front door. In those days, their parents used it as a way to make them accountable for their behavior. As they grew older, they used it as a safety precaution against the dangers in an unpredictable world.

Bernice had the last entry dated a few days earlier. Her tight, well-formed handwriting listed a man named Harvey Gulick, address and phone number and in parentheses, retired, met in church. Brenda rolled her eyes as she thought what a live wire he must be. In her flowery handwriting, she wrote on two lines: Alex Graves, tall, handsome, employed. Didn't he say he repaired computers at Circuit Depot? She had not confirmed that but who would make up a boring job like that. She scrolled down through her cell phone contacts, found his name, and wrote down his number into the book.

Not that she would admit it to Bernice, but she felt a little apprehensive about Alex. Comparing her entry to the one Bernice had written, she realized she did not know where Alex lived, his home number or even what model car he drove. Before tonight, they had met twice at Peg's Coffee Shop downtown. Tonight he was taking her to Clancy's Surf and Turf. Even though she thought about asking him to pick her up, in the end she decided to meet him there.

Years of conditioning by their parents, and now by Bernice, had made her wary of strangers and their motivation. After giving it more thought, she convinced herself not to place so much emphasis on the trivial. It was only dinner, for Heaven's sake.

The waiter seated her at a candlelit table by the window. Brenda kept her hands busy with a glass of Chardonnay. Judging from their last two meetings, Alex was usually prompt but still had not arrived. After another fifteen minutes, she finished the wine and pulled her phone from her purse. Her mixed emotions fluctuated between embarrassment and indignation aggravated by the wine. She pressed send, and listened to the ringing of his phone echo beside her.

"I'm sorry I'm so late. Forgive me," Alex said, leaning in from behind her.

Flushed from her thoughts seconds ago and aroused by his breath on her ear and neck, she felt herself regressing into an inexperienced teenager.

"That's okay," she said. "I had a glass of wine while I waited."

"Good. I'm glad you're not mad. I was heading out the door at work when my boss called me back in."

"We have the rest of the evening. This restaurant has a good reputation. I'm looking forward to it," Brenda said. "Was anything wrong?"

"What do you mean?"

"At work. You said your boss called you back in so I thought there might be a problem."

"Nothing, really. Stock has disappeared and management wants to figure out if it's customers or employees. They're asking everyone to volunteer to take lie detector tests starting tomorrow."

"Is that legal?"

"It's not mandatory," Alex said. "Anyway, let's not worry about that tonight. We're supposed to be here for a good time."

Alex had an edge in his voice that told her to leave that subject alone, but no matter how she tried, the idea that Alex had been asked at all bothered her. After a cup of coffee with their desserts, the waiter brought the black leather bill holder and placed it in front of Alex before discreetly backing away. Alex reached first into his right pant pocket, then the left. He felt in his jacket pockets and looked over at her with surprise.

"I can't believe this. My wallet is missing," he said.

"What? Is it in your car?"

"No. Anyway, I remember I had it at work. I must've taken it out for the coffee machine and set it on my desk. Oh, my God. I'm embarrassed to ask you this, but can you pay for the meal? I'll write you a check. We can go over to my office right now and get my wallet and checkbook. Heck, I might even have the cash."

Did she have an internal bullshit meter she had never noticed before? She tried to keep her tone light and friendly, just in case he was *not* lying. "No problem. These things happen." She pulled out her wallet and slipped her card into the sleeve of the bill holder. She smiled back at him, regarding his handsome features. It would not take much encouragement to fall into those deep brown eyes and lose herself for a few hours. "Don't be easy," is what her father used to say to her before her dates. Funny that he had not said that to Bernice, but she let that go. Tonight, if she were lucky, she *would* be easy. Wistfulness rushed over her and made her wonder how long it would take him to "work off" the $135.00 restaurant bill.

"While you take care of that, I have to go to the men's room. I'll be right back." He got up, and rushed away as she the waiter returned. After refreshing her coffee, the waiter took her card, went away to process the charges, and returned to her, but Alex still had not returned. She left a tip, hastily signed the credit card slip, and handed it back to the waiter. She replaced her credit card in her purse, and when she raised her head again, she saw Alex crossing from the other side of the dining room.

"Thank you, Madame," the waiter said before leaving the table without looking at Alex. Brenda wondered if this was some *man* thing—one man avoiding a direct look at another when one felt either embarrassment or disapproval of the other.

"Sorry I took so long. I made a call to be sure I could get into my office. I'd hate for you to drive me out there to find we couldn't get in."

"What about *your* car?"

"Um, it's at the mechanic's shop. I got a ride here from someone at work."

Brenda brushed off an uneasy twinge. "So, we're good to go?"

"Yep," Alex said. "Oh, wait a minute. Why don't you go

out and get your car. I want to make a call to my brother and it's a little private. It'll only take a minute and I'll meet you out front."

"Sure," Brenda said. This romantic evening was not turning out to be very romantic with him arriving late, forgetting his wallet, and leaving her on own so long. What next? Babysitting?

Brenda drove to his office, feeling the evening was finally getting interesting when she felt a warm hand reach around her neck. He pulled her into a kiss while they sat at a red light. Using all of her self-control to focus on the task of driving, she was happy when he directed her to turn in through the open driveway of a fenced property.

Inside a larger industrial park with business condominium units and warehouse offices, the road lead them to a massive brick structure surrounded by a second tall fence topped with barbed wire. When she stopped in front of the closed gate, Alex jumped out. "I'll open the gate."

She squinted to watch him working on something she assumed had to be a combination lock. He stopped and stood back to watch the massive gate as it began to slide to the left. He got back in the car, and motioned her to drive through the gate and around the back where loading dock platforms lined up along the entire back of the building.

For a moment, Brenda envisioned becoming a murder victim found in an isolated spot just like this, but she shook off the thought. All this was a temporary glitch in what she hoped would be an eventful evening. Sure, she had doubts when she had to pay for dinner, but he was going to make it right. That is why they were here.

"Pull over to the back end of the parking lot," Alex said, pointing to a dark area at the side of the building.

"This is spooky. Why can't I park in the lighted area?"

"When the security guard comes around, he might think you don't belong here and call the cops. By the time everything gets straightened out, our evening will be shot," he whispered, and reached over to kiss her again.

"Just hurry. I've seen too many scary movies and I have a wild imagination."

"I'll remember that later." He winked at her and left the car.

Brenda leaned back and allowed her mind to wander to thoughts of later at his place. By the end of the evening, they would no longer be strangers. They would have discovered the nuances of each other's body by touch and taste until she they fell exhausted into a contented oblivion.

Between the wine and the late hour, she became drowsy and closed her eyes. She realized she must have dozed off when she woke up with a jolt, cold and confused. She opened her eyes, not sure how long she had been waiting. Her watch display said 1:45 am, but she knew that had to be wrong. They had arrived close to 11:00. A quiet stillness surrounded her as she rolled down the window and listened.

Uneasiness came over her. At times like this, she had an inconvenient habit of doing the opposite of what hindsight would later tell her should have been the right action. Trying to come to the decision about what to do next, she weighed her choices. The smartest thing would be to call 911 and let the police look for Alex. Or *was* that the smartest thing, she asked herself as she realized how suspicious her presence here was without Alex to corroborate. She could wait and do nothing, but that meant ignoring that something might be wrong. Besides that, she had to pee. The obvious choice was to get out of the car and look for Alex. One problem with that was if someone had hurt Alex, he would most likely do the same to her. The other problem with that was she had no key to the building, and from her obstructed view, had not even seen the entrance he had used.

What would Bernice do? That answer was quick. Bernice would not be here in the first place. Maybe she should call her. No, Bernice would scold her and tell her to get the heck out of there. Looking down at her phone, she scrolled through her address book on the verge of calling her sister, but when she saw the photo of Alex, she selected his name instead, and pressed the green phone key. Then she waited.

She listened to the ringing and wondered if he might be ignoring her, or maybe the reason is that he could not answer. She broke through her nervousness, and knew what she had to do. She had misgivings about getting out of the car, but she considered how wrong it would be to drive off only to find out later that she left Alex to die. How would she feel if he were still alive, but died because no one had found him in time? So much time had passed, that she might still be too late already.

"What the hell." She opened the car door, jumped out, and ran to the back of the building.

She checked each bay for unlocked entry, until she came to an employee entrance. The door with metal crisscrossing threads imbedded in its thick glass interior allowed her a view of a long interior wall. The door gave in to her push. She hesitated before making the decision to walk inside.

"Yoo-hoo. Alex, are you here?" Her whispered voice, sounding unnatural and unfamiliar, echoed through the silence of the hall. She cleared her throat and called out in a louder voice, "Alex, please answer me. Are you in trouble?"

The building interior remained still and lifeless; her interior was anything but that.

She moved forward into the sterile environs where its fluorescent light cast a sterile haze into every corner. Her heart thumped in violent beats as sweat formed in inconvenient places under her clothes. She grabbed the first doorknob on her left. She had meant to call his name but no sound came out when she tried. She finally admitted that she was petrified.

That was when she knew that if he were here, he must be dead. She had called out his name when she came in and heard nothing. *Stands to reason.* Not for the first time in her life would she talk herself into the easy way out. That meant deciding that Alex was not hurt and had left her. She started to back herself toward the exit.

The distance back to the door seemed further and took longer than it did going in reverse. Every fiber of her body tingled from fright, alert to every sound, aware of every shadow. With her nerves like bare live wires, the paralyzing fear that made her want to stay in one spot lost out only to the more rational concern that someone might find her there and harm her. With a burst of decisiveness, she ran down the short hall through the door and around the building to her car.

To her relief, the car keys were still there. She turned on the ignition, locked the doors, and put the heat on full blast before turning the car around and leaving through the still-open gate. The idea of leaving that gate open worried her, but this was a matter of life and death. *That's the position I'll take if anyone asks me.* She rehearsed her story in case a security guard noticed her or stopped her.

By the time she turned onto her street, she realized how angry she was. Sure, she was spitting mad at Alex for ditching her, but not as mad as she was at herself. If Bernice ever heard about this, there would be no end to her lording it over her for the rest of their lives. How could she be so taken in?

At three o'clock, she pulled into the driveway. She left the car in front of the garage to avoid the noise of the garage door opening. Bernice would be sure to hear it and come out to interrogate her on coming home so late. Creeping along the side of the house to the entrance by the laundry room, she estimated she could go in this way quietly and unnoticed. Bernice slept on the other side of the house and would not hear. Just as she had settled onto her bed and was taking off her shoes, her cell phone rang. Her choice of ring tone sounded like reveille as it reverberated through the house. She made a mental note to change it in the morning, grabbed it quickly, and flipped it open.

"This better be good," she said.

"Listen, babe. I'm sorry to have left you there, but I had no choice," Alex said.

"I can't believe you have the nerve to call me," said Brenda. Now, she stung with the humiliation that he had not been hurt, but that he had just abandoned her. Her emotions started to rise to the surface, but she would not let him know she had been scared. She stuffed down her anger so she could speak without crying.

"Maybe I'm a real dirt bag, but I have to let you know what happened for your own good."

"What are you talking about? I hope you're not going to tell me you left me alone in a deserted parking lot to save me from zombies."

"No. I'm telling you that my friends and I robbed that place last night. I put sleeping pills in your wine and I didn't imagine you'd wake up before I got back. You were supposed to be my alibi. Since you did wake up and left, I thought I should tell you in case the police contact you."

"Are you kidding me? I don't know how to respond to that confession, except that I'm not protecting you. You really *do* have gall!"

"I don't care what you think. Tell the police what you want, like it will do you or them any good." Then the call shut off and was gone.

She held the phone away from her ear, mouth gaping. "Holy Mother of God! What have I gotten myself into? How could someone do this to me?"

She reached for the small hand mirror she kept on her nightstand and studied her face. She looked tired. Her heavy mascara and eyeliner had left smudges under her eyes. Her skin tone from using the wrong foundation color looked washed out. Her hair, that earlier had an elegant style, looked coarse and disarranged. She had held high hopes for the night out with Alex. Maybe even something bordering on permanent. Now, she saw what reality looked like—an old woman, gullible and unwanted.

Expecting a knock on the front door any minute, she took a little blue Valium she had saved from her dental work. She crawled onto the bed with still wearing all of her clothes and make-up. Her tired eyes crusty and swollen from the residual mascara, but she did not care. She closed her eyes and fell into an exhausted and uneasy sleep.

Brenda wandered into the kitchen at ten o'clock the next morning with aching sinuses and bloodshot eyes. Bernice, sitting at the window reading the paper, gave her a disapproving look but did not comment. Brenda poured herself a large mug of coffee and set the sausage in the cast iron skillet to cook. She plopped into her usual seat across from Bernice, and grabbed the local news section from the paper.

"Looking for your obituary?" Bernice said.

"Kiss my ass," Brenda said.

"Don't you think you're a little old to drag yourself home at three o'clock in the morning?"

"Why don't you get a life and stop spying on me?"

Bernice looked at her with their mother's disapproving face. "It's not spying when you get woken up by rattling keys, creaking doors, and cell phone calls. I would prefer not to know how my sister is managing while she is going through her second childhood."

"Kiss off. I don't owe you an explanation for my actions."

Bernice tilted up her chin and grunted. "Maybe not, but I do have the right to expect you to respect that I live here too."

After looking through all the sections of the paper, Brenda finally found what she was looking for—an abbreviated story on the burglary details from the night before. She forced herself to read it, afraid of finding a description of her or her car at the scene. She heaved a sigh when she learned there had been no witnesses and no leads—this owing chiefly to the malfunctioning security cameras and the absence of the security guard who had been in a car accident on his way to work. The security company was taking responsibility for their faulty equipment, but the police did not suspect duplicity. The focus of the investigation was the employees because there was no sign of forced entry. Brenda breathed out a sigh of relief that no one saw her there. At least she had escaped with most of her dignity.

With that worry behind her, she took a moment to look inwardly at her recent behavior. As unpleasant as it was to admit, Bernice knew her well and there was truth to what she had said. For all her fantasies of romance, travel, the high life that she had expected after their parents died, Brenda had experienced more frustration and doubt about herself than she had since her awkward preteen years. All the adventures she longed to experience looked better on paper than they did put into action, not to mention hidden risks when inviting strangers into your life. She knew that annoying person across the table had been right about her the whole time.

"Mind you, I'm not admitting anything, but I think I'm the one who needs to join a church choir, don't you?" She looked up at Bernice.

Reaching over to touch Brenda's hand, looking compassionate rather than judgmental, Bernice smiled, "We'd love to have you."

THE GOODS FACTORY

Paolo heard the metallic click of the deadbolt behind him in the cold darkness and knew he was in trouble. His first mistake had been leaving the key in the lock outside. His second mistake had been not finding the light switch before he let the door spring shut behind him. His third mistake had been standing too close to the threshold so that the door whacked him on the back, shoving him into the room as it closed. He scolded himself that a ten-year old should know better.

He stood motionless, and blinked to focus in the inky blackness of a room he knew had no windows. Pressing his small frame against the door, he pushed with the force of his small body to detect a give in the door, but met an unyielding barrier. A sudden ominous urgency crept over him that he had to find a way out of Aunt Ada's cold room. He could not let anyone know how foolish he had been.

Calculating how long it had been since he had eaten breakfast, an overwhelming odor struck his nose and jolted him out of his food fantasies. His panic must have distracted him from registering the heavy stink, so dense that each breath he drew was thicker than the last. The instinct to escape overtook him.. He turned and started to beat on the door, calling out for help. After a minute of frenzied pounding, he stopped short and ran his small fingers over and around the entire door until he confirmed what he already knew. No handle or knob on the inside, only the deadbolt lock, and its empty keyhole. His every nightmare was coming to life.

He placed a bent elbow over his nose and mouth hoping his short shirtsleeve would mask the smell. Using his free right hand to explore the room, he waved it around to feel for anything recognizable. Even in the absolute darkness, he closed his eyes to visualize the outside of this room built inside the barn-like garage.

Wood siding covered packed insulation over a self-constructed shed built of two-by-fours and Styrofoam. The rear of the cold room attached to the inside back wall of the garage, leaving three exposed sides. The front wall had the only door, a built-in air conditioning unit, and its control box. Above the door, an embossed metal sign with raised letters read, "Goods Factory." His only way out depended on finding a key.

His face turned toward the wall, he sidestepped to the right unsure of his footing, trying to identify what his hand touched as he inched along. He patted the wall up and down in cautious movements, and then left to right until his fingers recognized pegboard. His dad hung cutting tools in their garage on a similar wall. He withdrew his hand, hesitant to chance cutting his fingers on sharp-edged tools that might hang here. His hand moved down to meet a wooden workbench and its shelves below that held nothing within his reach. He stooped over to sweep around his vicinity for anything in his path.

By making slow, deliberate movements, he arrived at the corner of the room and touched a stool tucked in the narrow space between the workbench and a larger worktable on the adjacent wall. He turned around and used both hands for stability to hop onto the wooden seat. Now deeper into the room, the intensity of the smell overtook his senses. He held back involuntary gagging and returned his left arm back over his face.

He sat still, relieved from the tension of the last several minutes. This gave him time to calm down long enough to reason out his situation. He wondered what his dad would do if this happened to him, but decided this would not happen to his dad—he was too smart. And he knew what his dad would say to him. 'Use your head, boy. You can figure it out.' *Easy for him to say*. The weight of the smell bore down the back of his throat made him want to gag.

A tear crept out from the corner of his eye as he played out humiliating scenarios to come. *What if Mom calls the police because she thinks I'm missing?* He flinched hearing the adults snickering about the messes kids get into as if he were not there. Then, his mother's words came to him when she had warned, "A prideful heart will be your downfall," her interpretation of "Pride goest before destruction," from Proverbs that he learned about in Sunday school. Its meaning came rushing over him how his certainty that he could enter and leave here without anyone knowing was pride, and his destruction was to die in here like a trapped animal. His stomach spasmed with fear and he heard himself weeping. Knowing Mom was right again did not make him feel better.

When it came down to blame, he decided if Aunt Ada had not told him the Goods Factory was off-limits, he would not be here now. That mysterious room inside the garage about the size of his bedroom had occupied his thoughts since he its construction. Always locked, he never had the chance to see what she kept inside, and she had dismissed him when he showed interest. She had said that whatever she had inside was nothing for a young boy and that he should never go in there.

The frequent times he had been alone raking leaves or taking her garbage cans to the alley, he had tried to find a key without success. He did not care if she would call it snooping. He had to know the big secret. He had two weeks before she came back from vacation to look for a way in and he had been lucky. At least, he had thought so at the time when he found the key hanging on a small hook high on the back wall of the garage. Overcome by the excitement, he had inserted the key, swung open the door, and walked inside without thinking.

Sitting in the dark, suffocating from the smell now mixed in his own nervous sweat, he grudgingly admitted that this could be his fault. Yet, he refused to give up the notion of himself as a victim, even if a victim of his own crime. As if on cue, he heard the warning voice of his mother say, "God sees everything all the time, not only while we pray or go to church." Knowing that lying to others is easier than lying to himself, the painful deliverance stung his face, bringing on an uncontrollable stream of tears.

"Please, God, if you get me out of here, I will never do anything like this again," Paolo said, his raised head, his eyes closed, and his small hands pressed together. Hearing his voice praying made him feel better, and he was sure he and God could work something out once he admitted he had learned his lesson.

His confidence surged believing in his imminent escape, so he returned to the problem of the persistent odor. The thick, biting stench had grown stronger as he moved further away from the door. The source of the smell must be near. If he could find out what caused it, he could do something, but that smell did not make it easy to think.

He concentrated on the character of the smell as his dad had taught him. He listed the identifiable qualities on his mental blackboard—wet, thick, putrid, nasty. Like the time he had walked past the homeless guy at the park who had thrown up on himself. A confusing sweetness occurred to him at the same time, but a sweetness that repulsed him rather than attracted him as candy did. The thickness in the air of the room coated his skin and penetrated his clothes and hair. A sickening pall engulfed him once he believed he understood what he smelled—the rotting remains of a corpse.

Positive now, recalling the conversation he had heard while hiding behind the shrubbery listening to his dad's friends talk about the smell of dead bodies. The particular incident stuck out in his mind because for the first time he understood that his own dad was a cool doctor who handled dead people, like on television. Paolo had listened as his dad described witnessing an autopsy of a woman who had been dead three days before her neighbors found her.

"Just like the smell when my wife left raw hamburger on the counter that she forgot to take with us on a three-day camping trip. When we walked into this house, well, I don't know what's worse." He could still hear the men laughing at the story. Paolo had been embarrassed to admit to his parents why he refused to eat meat the following week.

His hands trembling and his insides quivering, he tried not to breathe in the foul air, but he grew dizzy holding his breath. His dad told him that people faint because they get scared and don't realize they're not breathing. He knew he needed to breathe, but he thought that if he did, he would throw up. All he could think to do was to lift off his favorite Phoenix Suns tee shirt, and tie it at the back of his head to cover his nose and mouth. Better than before but the smell still filtered through when he expanded his chest to suck in the air.

He was positive he had stumbled onto a murder, so his escape was more important. He had to get out to tell the police. They would know what to do.

Paolo slid off the stool to move further into the room to find the body. The darkness amplified the stench into a macabre manifestation of a presence hovering close. The heroics he imagined a moment before faded the more he pictured the rotting remains that occupied the room with him. Putrefying gases, disintegrating skin exposing the deteriorating flesh, set aside as part of a cunning plot still unknown.

The meaning of the "Goods Factory" had a new and frightening meaning, likely referring to human body parts Aunt Ada carved up before or after their death. He wondered if she went away to kill someone new and if she had murdered Uncle John. Worse than that, she would kill him to keep him quiet. Every nerve in his body burned as if on fire. His heart pounded in his chest with such ferocity, his neck and ears throbbed.

His two small hands reached out and found the wall again.

Touching nothing but the textured surface, he followed the worktable to his right. Metal, smooth, and cold, he forced his fingers to glide across the rounded end of the table and up onto its top. His slow-moving fingertips slid to the center until he touched something sticky. He jumped away, and he heard a squawk come from his mouth that echoed and sounded artificial.

He gave into his first instinct, and lifted his sticky fingers to his nose and regretted it. He had found what smelled and stuck it right up to his nose. His next instinct to get the smell of the gooey substance off his fingers resulted in a new mistake—rubbing his hands on his pants. Tempted by the thought of removing his pants, he decided to keep investigating and hope he could stand it.

He passed that worktable, and found another smaller table made of a thick wooden slab and thick round legs. No stickiness on this one. He reached over to feel the wall, and he touched metal hooks dangling from a cross bar and jerked his hand away in terror calculating their size could hold a body his size. He used every ounce of self-control to concentrate on staying calm while the beads of sweat ran down his forehead and into his eyes.

He moved to his right, stopping at the corner to feel around on the bare walls. As he started to turn to his right, he ran into a large object he recognized as a deep freezer. The steady hum, now obvious, he had mistaken for the air conditioner. The pieces fell into place for him—this is where she keeps the dead bodies!

His body tingled half from excitement and half from a terror that he had never imagined. He moved his hands, palms down across the freezer surface in sideways sweeps. The smell had grown so intense that it could have been a form hovering in front of him. The shirt over his nose and mouth provided no protection now. Halfway across, his right hand butted into a large, sticky mass, the right size for a torso.

He gasped so hard, he could not breathe as tightness started to suffocate him. He moved his hands away, turned around, and leaning against the freezer's front side, let his body slide down to the floor. Noxious sweat seemed to pour from under his arms, and his bladder fluttered as if he would pee. Instead, his breakfast came up in one large eruption that heaved him forward.

His shirt, once providing protection from the stench, added the smell of vomit to an already unbearable odor. He yanked the shirt off his head, wiped his mouth on a dry part and tossed it into the dark void. Shaking and weak, he leaned back against the offensive appliance and started to cry. The oppressive darkness of the odor smothered him, and he gave into the defenseless paralysis, resigned to his fate. No longer caring if anyone caught him crying, he escaped into an exhausted unconsciousness as his body sank to the floor where he crumpled into the fetal position.

He could not tell how long he had been asleep when he heard a key turning the deadbolt lock. His path to freedom! But as quickly as he embraced that joy, he grew afraid again. His rescue depended on whose face he saw on the other side of the door. He heard the final turn of the key that released the deadbolt. His senses raw, his body aching, time moved in dizzying slow motion. He remained motionless, except for the racing pulse in his throat. He put himself into a squat on shaking knees, his palms down on the floor. He squinted to focus as he saw the first crack of light from behind the moving door. He held his breath, willing himself to stay conscious.

He surprised himself when the door opened halfway. He jumped up and ran as fast as he could, pushing his way through the door. He registered the difference in momentum when the door shoved the person behind it backward. Wild and crying again, his mouth babbling, his unseeing eyes not yet adjusted to light, he could not decide on a direction for the best route for escape.

Before he could move in any direction, a pair of arms grabbed him around his naked waist to stop him. Squirming to get away, he calmed down when his mind registered that the person speaking in the familiar voice was his mom.

"My poor baby, what on earth happened to you? You're white as a ghost and you smell like the devil."

The amusement in her eyes looked demonic through his distorted vision. "This isn't funny, Mom. Aunt Ada is a serial killer. I found a body. The smell in there is awful." Breathless, he wrapped his arms around his mother's small frame with such strength, she had difficulty extricating herself from his grip.

"Show me what you saw," she said. Her soft, melodic voice, sounded so calm and ordinary, he wondered if he had dreamt it all.

"Okay," he said. Taking her hand, his bravery and strength returned. He pulled her back to the doorway where she reached for the light switch he had missed by the pegboard. The flicker of the fluorescent light followed by its full brightness provided him the first view of the interior of the Goods Factory, but he did not follow her inside.

"Tell me what you saw."

"I didn't *see* anything. I felt something sticky and gross on the metal table, and the part of a body on the freezer."

When he saw her sympathetic face, she said the last thing he expected to hear.

"Mommy's brave little soldier. You must have been frightened out of your wits. That smell is awful, isn't it? But it's not what you think. Come here and look." She took his hand, and gently pulled him inside the room. He was grateful she did not mention the streaks of vomit across the floor and his favorite shirt wadded in a ball against the wall. He walked over to stand beside her.

"You were close in what you thought you smelled."

"What I *thought* I smelled?"

"Sweetheart, what you smelled was rotten meat. The truth is the smells aren't too far apart. What I don't understand is where you got the idea in the first place, but never mind that for now. I told your father *The Twilight Zone* would give you nightmares and fuel that wild imagination of yours.

Paolo felt his face redden. He hated to be wrong and hated

more to look foolish.

"Aunt Ada and Uncle John were butchers and had a small butcher shop in Sunnyslope Plaza called the Goods Factory. Remember two years ago, the day after your seventh birthday, when we went to watch the demolition? Then, a few months ago, we went to the Brookshire Restaurant for the last meal before they tore that down, too?"

No, he did not remember, but he knew grownups believed children remembered their important events and looked shocked when they did not. "I guess I forgot."

"Their shop was in between the Ben Franklin Store and the Rexall Drug Store, at the opposite end from the AJ Bayless. Now the strip is the hospital parking lot for the Emergency Room. Remember where we went when you broke your leg?"

He nodded, recalling another embarrassing misadventure.

"John and Ada retired when the stores were torn down. At their age, they said it was too much effort to start over somewhere new, especially once supermarkets started popping up everywhere. Instead, they kept some of the equipment for their workshop at home. They built this refrigerated room to butcher and keep meat they bought or hunted."

Paolo looked around the room, smaller than it seemed in the dark. What had terrified him minutes before now a harmless stainless steel commercial kitchen, like the back of a restaurant.

"Come here," she said. He went to stand next to her and she laid her arm on his shoulders. "I think age might have gotten to Aunt Ada. She didn't cut this leg of lamb like she usually does. I think in the middle of butchering her meat, something interrupted her, and then she forgot to come back to finish the job and clean up the blood. Getting ready for her trip, the whole thing slipped her mind, poor thing. Like I did when we went camping last year and I forgot the meat."

"Gee whiz, I remember that. Dad tells that story a lot. But why didn't she want me in here?"

"Oh, son of mine, is that what all this is about? Because you were curious? I always say your curiosity is a curse on commonsense! Aunt Ada didn't want you in here because of safety issues. Too many sharp objects. Look, bone saws, meat hooks, butcher knives, bone scrapers. All things little boys should not be handling without an adult around ."

"I'm sorry, Mom. I thought she had a hidden treasure and I wanted to see. Gosh, I feel real dumb. Everyone's going to laugh at me.," He struggled to hide his emotion-choked voice.

"No one's going to know about it. The first thing we're going to do is to clean up this mess. You know where Ada keeps her plastic trash bags. Go get two big green ones."

Turning his focus on an activity made the time in the cold room seem far away. He rushed back with the bags, and then watched while she grabbed the rotting meat with hands covered by the first bag and dropped it into the second. She produced disinfectant and paper towels, and wiped away the congealed blood. Then, she turned to the job of cleaning the floor. Paolo used paper towels to pick up his vomit and folded up his tee shirt and tossed both in with the bag with the meat. Without the offensive substances, he breathed clean air again. His earlier experience grew faint and distant, like one of his nightmares—gone in the daylight.

"I'm going to tell Aunt Ada that you noticed the smell and told me, so I came over to check on it and together we cleaned up the mess. This will be our secret, so don't tell your father. I don't want you to think it's okay to lie, but he would punish you. After seeing your face when you ran out of here, I think you've been punished enough. I'm also sure you've learned your lesson about what comes from being too curious. Right?"

"Gee, thanks Mom. You're the best."

"I know, but we'll keep that our secret, too. We can't let your dad know I'm that nice," she said giving him a wink and a hug before they walked through the backyard gate to the alley where she heaved the rotten remains into the depths of the communal trash bin.

After locking the door to the Goods Factory, and then the garage, the two walked through the house and out the front door. Paolo pulled it closed behind them and used his key to lock up. He took a second to look skyward and formed the words 'thank you, God' before catching up to his mother. He laughed thinking that for the first time, he looked forward to a bath.

Inside, a peaceful quiet had settled over the Goods Factory. The humming motor a soothing lullaby for the unopened freezer that stood guardian of its contents with the exception of the strands of grey hair caught in its hinge.

WOMAN'S WORK

Sipping her coffee and watching the other five around the table doing the same, Josefina was startled when she heard the soft wind rattle the water bucket hanging outside the kitchen door. Winter in Flagstaff was harsh compared to the temperate climate of her León in Mexico, and by its bleak nature, propelled her further into a sense of isolation and nervousness. Before she recovered, she heard another gust of wind whistle through the Ponderosa pines before slamming metal tools against the wood rack where they hung outside the garden shed.

The familiar sounds fueled an already tense atmosphere that Josefina saw on the faces of her husband, Ricardo, and their friends. In the nearby distance, she heard the comforting gentle snorts of the horses stabled in the structure across the yard.

Kerosene lamps scattered around the room and centered on the table, they leaned inward as if to keep warm even though the parlor stove was the primary heat source. The cooking stove upstairs in the kitchen and the parlor stove in the front room made the ground floor cozy this time of year, but down here in the basement, the penetrating coldness of the earth left a chill that made her bones ache.

"Are we all agreed to leave everything as it is for now?" The sound of her husband's voice brought her to the moment. "It's nineteen twenty. Times have changed. Not as easy to rob the stagecoaches and trains as it once was." Nodding in agreement, she knew she should pay more attention, but with the three men making all the decisions for their wives, she wondered what was the point.

Life had grown dull and her apathy had increased during the last couple of years. Compared to fighting with the *Soldaderas* in Mexico and supporting the soldiers behind the lines during the Revolution, the safe life of an American wife and mother in modern day Flagstaff was tame. No reason to run out in a fire spray of bullets to rescue soldiers, to shoot at the enemy with the two *pistolas* she had always carried, or to dress up as a man and fight in direct combat with the enemy. The security of her new life was to her a prison instead of a safe haven. At least the thrill of their daylight robberies of the stagecoaches and trains, made her feel alive. Now, as Ricardo had promised, that would stop and the six, with their children, would forget that life and settle into comfortable positions in this community.

Grinning at her own imagination, she found that visualizing shooting out Ricardo's kneecaps for sticking her here gave her a sense of justice and lightened her mood. At least enough to be civil after the others went home.

"What are you thinking about now, woman? I don't trust that sneaky smile you get sometimes," Ricardo said.

"Remembering the old days, that's all."

"The old days from two years ago, you mean. When we barely got out with our lives and had to sleep on dirt holding our guns? We did what we had to do and now we don't need to live like that anymore. I think the real problem is you got used to having that power and you miss it," he said pointing his forefinger between her eyes. "Well, society women are pampered and delicate and make their concerns the needs of their men and their children. They don't shoot people and ride horses bareback, and they sure don't rob stagecoaches. You need to get over that and get on with what God intended for you as a woman."

"Women are going to get the vote any day now. That is what God intended or it would not happen."

"It hasn't happened yet, has it? What a world that would be. Every woman cancelling out her husband's vote. That's not moral. I want to know what those Suffragists are up to anyway, taking over the world?"

"Yes. We want to take over the world and when we do, you'll be the first to go!"

Her next thought was how handy her pistol was hanging inside the cold closet, followed by the amusement of his shocked face when she shot him. As pleasing as the fantasy was, she would never kill him. Her children were not going to suffer the humiliation of knowing their mother was hanged for anything, much less for killing their father. He was right about one thing. The person she hid inside had no place in society now. Maybe things would change in her lifetime.

Waking up the next day, Josefina opened her eyes to a clear, crisp morning. Even with the brisk temperature, the sun was strong and warming. With Ricardo packing up to head to Phoenix for banking and the children sent to school in San Francisco for the winter break, Josefina speculated that the day before her could be a soothing break or a monotonous bore. Icy windowpanes stung her fingers when she leaned in to survey her property and the surrounding neighborhood. A dusting of early morning snow deadened sounds on the street surfaces until the sun reached down to melt it, while the other homes seemed to draw themselves inward out of defense from the frigid winds.

"Leavin'," Ricardo said.

Smiling, she followed him downstairs to the kitchen and down the stairs to the basement door where they said their goodbyes. Her eyes followed him as he rode off down the hill and out of her sight. One day, she thought, they would get a horseless carriage. Then she could go with him on these trips.

Alone in the house, enjoying coffee before the morning

chores, she had a start when she heard the basement door leading to the back yard open and shut. An unfamiliar pierce of fear shot through her midsection and froze her. Could Ricardo have returned? Before she had time to react, a man burst through the door in the kitchen that lead to the basement stairs aiming a gun at her.

"What do you want?" Josefina's dark eyes glassy with the jolt of adrenaline held his glare.

"Don't ask questions. Fix me something to eat."

"You break into my house for food?"

"Shut up, and get to cookin'."

His eyes, his manner, his agitation, the face of desperation was familiar to Josefina. She had seen it before in Mexican soldiers. A need to escape from someone scarier than themselves meant they were reckless and dangerous, willing to do whatever they had to do to get out alive. She understood because she had lived it and knew the last thing she should do was to antagonize him. Suspicious eyes followed her as she went to the icebox and opened its right door to get eggs and bacon.

"What's in the other door? Open it." He used his pistol to point to the left side of the oak cabinet.

Moving to the right side of the icebox, she reached over to swing open the oak door that concealed the ice cabinet and drip pan.

"Never saw one of them fancy iceboxes. Okay, get on with it."

Using the cast iron skillet resting on the back burner, she dropped several slices of bacon to its warmed surface before turning to him. "Fire's low this time of day. Not hot enough to make a meal. I need more wood for the cook stove. It's outside the back door." With watchful eyes and his gun trained on her, she said, "Need more for the parlor stove too or this house will be as cold as it is outside."

"Get it and don't try nothing." He watched as she carried in an armful of logs, tossed one inside the cook stove, and the rest in a basket in the corner.

"Quit stalling and get on with it," he said.

Turning her attention to him from time to time, she continued cooking. Her advantage here was he probably assumed she was ordinary. With her five-foot frame, dark skin and round brown eyes, he would expect a feminine reaction. Taking solace in the belief she was too terrified to run, he would be confident that he could frighten her into submission. To keep him calm, she pretended to be afraid and intimidated. That would give him the feeling of dominance and would give her time to figure out how to handle him.

That Ruger pistol hidden in the cold closet was her best bet. Her problem was getting to the closet, grabbing the gun, pulling back on the hammer, all before he had time to react. If she were clumsy about it, she would not make it across the room before he shot her in the back.

While she took the bacon out of the skillet, she glanced over to find him looking not at her but out the window. So, she figured, he must be waiting for someone or was afraid of someone coming for him. This gave her a sense of urgency. One way or another, she had to deal with him before someone else showed up, and left her to subdue two men instead of the one.

Once the eggs had cooked, she dished up the food onto a tin plate and headed to the table. Keeping his gun aimed in her direction, his red-rimmed eyes darted from his plate to her as he started shoveling in food, swallowing without chewing.

"What's your name, woman?"

"Josefina."

"Where's your husband?"

"In town tending to business."

"You're a liar, Josefina," he said, speaking her name as a vulgar sound.

"He *is* tending to business."

"I saw him ride off, packed for a longer trip. It don't matter anyhow."

"Why did you pick my house? Why come up the hill when you could've stopped somewhere else."

"Simple. I saw your man leaving. Easier to handle a woman on her own."

Repressing an urge to laugh, Josefina kept her face soft and averted her eyes. She remembered Ricardo telling her she had dangerous eyes, and maybe she did. Dark, round, and piercing, the downward slant of her eyebrows expressed a deliberate sadness that could turn to anger in a flash.

An answer was not coming to her about what to do. Eventually, she would have to show her hand.

"Give me some of that coffee you got brewing there," he said, pushing away his empty plate and placing his gun in front of him. She poured his coffee and carried the large handled metal cup to the table. "Don't try anything with that boiling coffee or you won't live the seconds it takes to set it down."

"We're out of milk," she said, careful not to spill the hot liquid.

"Thought you'd be more scared. You're fair steady for a woman. Why is that?"

"Being careful, that's all. I don't want you to hurt me."

She continued avoiding eye contact with him and retreated to her place by the stove. She imagined that the old cur would think she was keeping her woman's place ever ready to serve the menfolk, and saw she was right when he relaxed long enough to sip the hot liquid. Sure he felt in control of her and the house, she waited for an opportunity to use that against him. First, she had to get her pistol from the cold closet.

"We might have milk in the cold closet over there."

"Okay. Git it."

Opening the door that concealed the cold closet, she reached in for a glass bottle of milk. Inside to the left, on a long nail hung her pistol that she kept loaded for emergencies. She turned her hip inside and knocked the Ruger into her apron pocket. A movement so swift, the only discernible clue was a new weightiness in her apron. When she brought out the milk, she walked to the stove and grabbed the dishtowel that she tucked into the waist of her apron, covering the sagging pocket. First step done, she thought, as she splashed milk into his cup.

As time passed, she developed a growing sense of urgency. Not knowing why he had to hide here and who or what he waited for, she started to give in to anxiety. Before she let that happen, she had to catch him off guard or take his mind off her long enough for her to get a shot. Do something that only a half-witted woman would do facing danger and sure death. Take some action to make him believe she behaved like a desperate female who acted without thinking of the consequences.

As if she had lost her mind, she started screaming for help at the top of her lungs. The impact had the effect she wanted. He lost his concentration and his temper, rushed over to her stumbling against the chair. He grabbed her by the arm, and slapped her across the face with, she was certain, the full force of his rage.

The blow sent her sliding across the floor. "Stupid woman," he said as he turned his back on her. Good, she thought, feeling the sting on her face from his rough hand. The assault made it easier to do what she had to do.

Rolling onto her back, she reached into her apron pocket and brought out the gun. Using both hands, she straightened her arms, locked her elbows, aimed, and pulled back the hammer. She saw him flinch in recognition as he heard the double-click the same time she did, but he could not react fast enough before she pulled the trigger.

Josefina watched the bullet make contact between his eyes, and then fired again in his left shoulder to make her shots appear wild for the benefit of the sheriff. The first shot jerked his head backward. The second shot dropped him in a heap.

A moment later, a dead man at her feet, she heard the sound of a single horse approaching fast, followed by an abrupt stop. After the sound of dismount, she heard her basement door open and shut for the third time that day. Annoyance mingled with anxiety, the adrenalin rush set her heart pounding and sharpened her mental acuity. She bent down to pick up the dead man's gun. She hid behind her kitchen's basement door and held his gun in firing stance. Heavy footsteps on the stairs grew louder. Tense, almost without breathing, she stood motionless as the door opened slowly.

The man coming through the door was cautious, but he moved with purpose into the kitchen without looking behind him. Josefina saw him recoil when he saw the dead man and raise his hand to his gun. Coming out from the back of the door, she slammed it closed with the bottom of her foot, took aim, and fired. A well-worn veteran of the outlaw class swung around in time for her to watch his surprised expression at the oncoming bullet.

Keeping her concentration and her calm, Josefina took his gun from its holster, and let it drop to the floor at his side. Rushing over to the first intruder, she returned his gun next to his hand. Her heart pounded through her clothes, and for the first time in hours, she felt cold.

Expecting the law to arrive any minute, she grabbed her thickest shawl before opening the kitchen door. Relieved to hear horse hooves on the dusty snow-covered roads, she leaned against the wooden porch posts and hoped she looked like a convincing victim. If the sheriff knew the truth, he might start to figure out that none of the six were what they seemed.

After the sheriff and the undertaker had come and gone, Josefina sat at her kitchen table. Adding more wood to the cooking stove, she left its door open to feel the heat on her skin. Her worry about how to tell her story had been unnecessary, and she was amused at how they put it all together on their own. The two men, gentle and caring, had applauded her heroics. Portraying her as a defenseless woman lucky enough to know where her husband kept his gun and gusty enough to use it to defend her home and her honor, neither bothered to ask the penetrating questions they would have asked a man in the same circumstances.

At one point, she started to laugh, hiding her face in her

hands, leaving the sheriff to believe she was crying. For what it was worth, she was positive she had been taught a great lesson about complaining that her life no longer had adventure and danger. At the same time too, she thought maybe it is a great advantage to be underestimated.

LAST STAND

Standing at the top of the concrete stairs, Edna listened as Randy screamed. With sudden clarity, she knew a time was coming when she would give in to his pressure to let him back into her apartment just to end the torment.

After following her for months, the threatening phone calls and his humiliating appearances at work, she was numb. "Do you know how easy it is to believe a drunk stumbled and fell down a flight of stairs?"

Before he had time to react, she wound her foot around his ankle and yanked.

THE CORSAGE

ellie Blake woke with a start when she heard a noise in the kitchen. *Or had she been dreaming? Was hearing things another symptom of old age?* She raised her head off the pillow to listen, and squinted at the clock—two in the morning. *Must've been a dream.* She fell back onto her pillow and shut her eyes. Before she had time to fall back asleep, she heard something. She froze. Should she ignore it or get up to check out the problem? The noise could have been the draw of the heating system kicking on, but what if someone had broken in? Surely, no one could be interested in robbing her.

She slid her feet from under the covers and into her slippers, pulled her walker close, and moved toward the kitchen of her three-room apartment. She heard the noise again and called out, "What's going on out there?" Another slam, but no answer.

She had turned on every light in the apartment by the time she arrived in the kitchen. Nothing looked out of place. The cabinet doors were all closed and showed no sign they had been disturbed. She looked up at the air register and thought about using the broom handle to close it, but she needed leverage and decided she did not have the strength. She had a fever and nasal congestion that drew on her energy, but not so bad that she could sleep with this racket going on all night.

According to the microwave clock, she had been standing in the kitchen for five minutes waiting for the noise to happen again. Except for an abnormal chilliness, the room and its contents remained still. She decided to go back to bed and forget about it. She settled back under the covers. Then, she thought she knew what had happened. The sound must have come from a neighboring unit, but sounded louder than usual in the quiet of the night. Yes, that had to be it.

From her third-floor window, Nellie looked down on the people rushing by during their lunch break. She shook her head at the ones wearing shorts walking next to others wearing sweaters and coats. Dressing for a Phoenix winter could be challenging. Her own clothes were damp with sweat. She fanned herself. In the Arizona desert, the winter sun heated the windowpanes and created stifling warmth inside that contrasted sharply to the outside temperature. When she raised the window, the wintry air rushed in and swirled around her tiny shoulders. She shrunk away, wrapped her shawl at her neck, and threw the loose end across her back. Just enough to shield her chest while she enjoyed the freshness of the outside air.

Towering above her senior living building, industrial steel office structures shadowed the foot-travelers, and acted as windbreakers against the occasional windstorms that whipped down alleys and through breezeways. On the sidewalk below, Nellie watched as the people pulled their arms in close against a sudden harsh breeze. What did they think as they walked? Surely, much like she, they suffered the curse of memories and the risks of living too long with regrets—and the unpleasant consequence of suffering their own company.

She pressed her hands on the outside edges of her chair to raise herself, and then placed her empty coffee cup in the holder of her walker. She had started moving toward the percolator when she caught sight of the bureau out of the corner of her eye, and had a sudden urge to look inside its neglected drawers. No doubt her dreams of Matthew last night stirred up old memories. Grasping the handles of her four-wheeled walker, she lumbered across the room to the wingback chair, and eased down onto its soft cushion. She pulled the top drawer out as far as she could without disengaging it from the glide and began to study the contents she had not seen in years.

She sighed when she looked down into the dusty drawer at the disorganized assortment of photo albums, pressed flowers, and old perfume bottles. She pulled everything out until she found the letters he sent to her during his time in the military—and the last corsage still in its original box. She placed them on her walker's padded seat and went back to the table. Her doctor told her to be more active, but she found this simple effort more strenuous than she wanted to admit. Once she settled back in front of the window, she took time to catch her breath, and then untied the ribbon around the packet of letters.

She smoothed out the first letter in front of her and began to read his romantic prose while her fingers slid open the clear corsage box, its flimsy plastic now brittle from age. She lifted the delicate buds to her nose, and breathed in the musty fragrance of three white miniature roses. Every sniff of the tiny white petals ignited ancient memories and a lightheaded sentiment.

She closed her eyes, and went back to the evening he gave her the corsage. Despite the cross words that had passed between them earlier that week, they were going to the annual charity dinner for the hospital where he worked. He told her she looked as beautiful as the day they met and handed her the small box. Her joy had overshadowed his earlier talk about a divorce, nonsense coming from a man in mid-life crisis.

She held the withered petals against her nose, as if pretending could bring back their original fragrance. The draw of each breath transported her back forty years before to when she had been the happiest. Common sense told her to stop sniffing when the dust irritated her nose and throat, but she could not resist the lure of returning to that day.

She sighed and set the corsage on the table. She tried to preoccupy herself with her favorite shows and crosswords, but she could not resist a compulsion to look at small bundle, pick it up, brush it across her face, and sniff it. By the evening, her breathing had grown raspy and short, due, she was convinced, to the dust on the corsage. She hoped she had not picked up the flu. Her doctor had warned her that people her age needed to get the vaccine, but she told him she would rather not. Enough chemicals surged through her body as it was. One pill for her heart, another for her high blood pressure, another for sleeplessness, and another for vision. Enough was enough, she had told him. Now, she would have to listen to his speech about not taking his advice if her symptoms turned into something serious.

By eight o'clock, she had nestled in her bed, freezing from her sweat-soaked clothes cooled by the dry heat rushing from the wall registers. She guessed the doctor had been right. If she were not better by morning, she would call him. She closed her eyes and drifted off. Then, bang!

"Nellie, don't be afraid. It's only me."

"Matthew? My God, what are you doing here?" Nellie sat up to get her focus and squinted at his figure in the dark doorway. She reached for her cane and got out of bed to get a closer look at him.

"Don't worry. I'm not staying. A man likes to drop by to visit his wife now and then. Find out how she's managing without him. I didn't mean to bother you."

"I'm doing fine. That is, until you almost gave me a heart attack."

"How's our little girl? Has she missed me much?"

"What a fool question. Of course, she missed you. But Belinda's not little anymore. She's way past forty. Been married twice. Has one daughter named Patrice."

"That was the worst part about leaving, you know—

missing her grow up. Has she had a happy life?"

"Her first husband got killed by a drunk driver. That was a tough time, but I think she's happy now. She got married again. You'd like this one—a good man, especially the way he helped raise Patrice just like she was one of his own. They live out in Reading."

Nellie shifted to lean on her other foot for relief. "I can't stand long these days. Bad hip."

"I'm sorry to hear that, Nell. After everything we went through, I never wanted you to suffer."

"Fine words coming from a man who left me to fend for myself the last forty years."

"You were always a fighter. I knew you'd be alright."

Nellie turned back toward the bed. "I've got to get my rest. I have a bad cold. I get so tired these days. I need all my sleep."

"I'll leave you alone then."

"Matthew, it's been good seeing you."

The next morning, she felt worse. She tried to pull herself out of bed to reach the phone to call someone, but fell back into her pillow. Patrice stopped by so often, even though Nell tried to discourage her—something she regretted now. Then she heard the familiar knock and a key turning the tumblers of her door lock.

"Gran, it's me."

"I'm in here in bed."

"Oh my God, Gran. What's wrong? You look horrible," Patrice rushed to her side. "You should've called me. How long have you been sick?"

"Since yesterday. The flu is worse than I remember. I guess I should have listened to the doctor about that flu shot."

"It's a little late now. I think we should get you to the hospital. It might be the light in here, but I don't like your looks."

"No hospitals," Nellie said. "At my age, you can end up dead from exposure to sick people in a germ factory like that."

"But Gran…"

Nellie waved her hand. "No buts. If it's meant to be my

time, I'd rather just go under my own steam." She saw the concern in Patrice's face. "Don't worry. I'll be fine. All I need is a few nourishing meals to build up my strength."

"Okay, but if you're not better tomorrow, I'm having the paramedics come and get you."

"We'll see about that." Nellie scooted up in the bed against the pillows and sat upright, shoulders back, head held high.

Patrice pulled food out of the freezer and pantry. "I'm fixing your favorite chicken stew."

"Just what I need."

"I wish you'd get out more. Mom said she's invited you over for the weekend many times and you refuse."

"Nobody wants an old woman hobbling around, reminding them that old age is just around the corner."

"Who thinks like that? Not anyone we know, for sure."

"No one says it out loud, but they think it. It's easier to be around youth and all that represents—immortality, health, endless possibilities, the future. Old people are reminders that life is shorter than you think."

"Gosh, Gran. That's such morbid thinking."

"That's my point."

"You're wrong, you know. I think that's a dumb excuse for shutting us out."

Nellie looked at Patrice. "I'm sorry. I shouldn't have said anything. That knowledge comes soon enough to all of us. When you're my age, you'll look back on this conversation and understand."

Nellie saw Patrice's eyes redden and fill with tears.

Patrice stopped chopping the carrots, and looked at Nellie. "Gran, I don't want to think about you dying. You'll leave an empty hole in my heart that no one can fill."

"Come give Gran a hug." Nellie opened her arms and Patrice ran over to her. "If it really means that much to you, I'll come over for a weekend. Okay? Now stop crying. Don't let an old woman depress you."

"I love you so much, Gran. Don't ever leave me."

"I love you too, dear." Nellie smoothed out Patrice's hair,

kissed her on the forehead, and pushed her to stand up. They looked at each other for several seconds before Patrice went back to the kitchen counter and her meal preparations.

They watched movies on Nellie's VCR, enjoying the smells of simmering chicken and vegetables filling the apartment. Nellie noticed out of the corner of her eye that Patrice watched her. Whether Matthew's visit affected her or her sickness had, Nell recognized retreat in her attitude, placing distance between her and the rest of the world. Patrice's empathetic nature must be sensitive to that. Then she had to open her mouth about death. No wonder Patrice had that worried expression on her face. *It's a good thing I didn't tell her about Matthew's visit.*

"This stew is delicious, sweetheart," Nellie said. "I needed a good meal. I feel better already."

"Good. I've set up bowls in the fridge so all you need to do is warm them in the microwave. Remember what I said. If you're not better tomorrow, you're seeing a doctor one way or another. I'll be back in the morning to check on you." Patrice gave Nellie a long look before leaving. "I love you Grandma."

"I love you, too, sweetheart. See you in the morning. God willing." *Why did she say that?*

Nellie woke confused and disoriented. More loud bangs in the kitchen. Her heart raced, and breathing hurt deep inside her chest. She sat up and tried to make out movement in the dark. *Was Matthew back?* She pulled her robe around her, and let her feet find her slippers. *Forget the walker—she might need to wallop someone.* She grabbed her cane and made cautious steps to the bedroom doorway. There would be no decent sleep until she figured out a way to keep those cabinet doors from banging, and tried to think of what she had in the apartment that could fasten them shut.

When she reached the kitchen, she saw Matthew.

"Must you slam those doors? Being woken up by that sound is enough to kill me from shock."

"Nellie, I'm sorry but I had to come back. I miss you. I want us to be together again, like before."

"Matthew, you know that's impossible. Can't you move on like other people. When something's over, it's over."

"Nellie, please. We were meant to be together. You're still mad that I told you I wanted a divorce. I know that hurt you. I guess I'm like a million other men who start thinking of their family as a harness. Like when a man gets older and thinks of all those early dreams. He thinks that if it weren't for the responsibilities of a wife and children, he could've done so much. By the time I realized how wrong I was, it was too late and I lost you."

"Matthew. You've got to stop dwelling on the past."

"To me, it's like it happened yesterday."

"But it was forty years ago. I don't hate you anymore. I'm not even mad that you went away. If anything, you're the one who should be mad at me."

"I know you didn't mean it—not really. You were hurt, that's all. I knew you acted that way because you loved me."

"I'm happy you can be at peace about that. I'm not sure I'm ready to forgive myself."

Matthew came closer to her, and she shook from the sight of him. "We're going to be together again and I will make up for everything. Tell me that's what you want, too."

"It's been so long. I can't think about that now. I'm not well. I need to go back to bed."

"Nellie, please don't be scared. You never have anything to fear as long as I'm around."

"I'm not afraid. I'm confused. I would like to have another chance with you, but I don't know if I'm willing to give up what I have now."

"Everything to its own time, Nellie."

She turned from him and made her way back to bed. "I need to rest. I can't talk about this anymore tonight. Please go away."

"Okay, but I'll be back for you later."

Matthew had gone before she reached her bed. She sat up,

thinking about what he said and about her future, what future she had left on earth anyway. At her time of life, she did not expect happiness. If anything, she expected a reckoning. Could she be certain Matthew had forgiven her? Or that God had forgiven her? She had never uttered the words to a living soul. She could not believe the idea that she could go with Matthew now and be happy.

She rested back on her pillows and closed her eyes in the hope of dozing off, but a sudden wet cough jolted her achy chest. Her head pounded, and her body was flush from fever. Patrice would have her in an ambulance before she knows what hit her. The way she felt now, she looked forward to the hospital, but she hesitated to call 911 on her own. She had a nagging feeling there was something important to do first, but she drifted off and found herself dreaming about that night forty years ago.

Nell watched her younger self take the dress from the back of the door and model it for Matthew. She had forgotten feeling this light and happy—how she had danced around the room in her slip and stockings, playing peekaboo with her housecoat until she toppled him and they both fell onto the bed laughing.

Then the confrontation they had the week before came in front of her.

"Nellie," he had said, "you drive every bit of love out of a person until nothing's left."

"I'll never let you leave me."

"Don't be ridiculous. You have no choice."

Nellie considered going to the charity function a conciliatory gesture that meant he did not mean those cruel words. She told him as much as they were putting on coats to leave. Instead of the embrace she expected, he heaved a heavy sigh and shook his head. "Where did you get that idea? I know how much you enjoy these events and I wanted to take you one last time."

The truth felt like scorch marks on her face. He stood there, victorious over her. A rage came over her. She started to pound him in the chest with all her strength—over and over. He laughed at first, taunting her by grabbing at her wrists to stop her. But then she saw the bewilderment on his face. Then, an agonizing facial contortion. She stopped struggling against him when he clutched his chest with his right hand while his left hand flailed to break his descent to the floor.

"Get me the nitro," he said, gasping.

"Did you mean what you said?"

"What kind of question is that at a time like this? Get the nitro first and we'll talk."

Nellie stood motionless looking down at him, hating him with every furious fiber of her body, her face still biting from rejection. She backed away from him so he could not clutch her ankles. His face pleaded with her. She watched his helplessness with curiosity, questioning her sanity that she could remain apathetic. When he stopped moving, she went to the telephone, dialed 911 and sat down. Her eyes fell on the unopened corsage, sitting like an innocent bystander, a harsh reminder of what she wanted to believe. She shoved it into her keepsake drawer, wanting to forget, but not willing to toss it out either.

Now, she faced her shame. Letting her husband die like that was murder, at least in God's eyes. Matthew stood over her bed now and looked down at her. His face, so much like she remembered him, gentle and loving. He forgave her and wanted her again. He leaned down and spoke in her ear, "Are you ready now?"

"I believe I am. It only occurred to me that I've been biding my time, waiting for you to come back." She reached out for his hand, and let him lift her to him. She had a lightness and joy she had not experienced since that night forty years ago.

Everything in its own time, she thought, no longer feeling the draw of her physical existence.

UNGUARDED MOMENTS

Myra thought she would heave her afternoon snack of cheese curls and ice cream sandwiches when she saw the familiar car out front. Not another one of Al's unannounced visits, she groaned.

Myra's Golden Retriever Pepper followed at her heels as she scurried around her small house looking for the paperback novel that Al had lent her. "It's got to be here. Didn't I put it here on the shelf," Myra said into the dog's curious eyes. She noticed the stress-induced sweat beading in her armpits and its accompanying anxiety. "Oh, Pepper, where is it? He's waiting."

At last, she saw the tiny paperback resting on a pile of out-of-state newspapers in the corner by the television. Relief. She grabbed it and rushed to her front door where Al leaned against his idling car.

"Sorry about the wait, Al," said Myra. "To tell you the truth, I'd forgotten it. I finished reading it last week. I should've returned it you the minute I finished."

"No problem. I thought I'd make it easy and pick it up so you didn't have to bring it in to work."

"So, what're you doing on this side of town? I thought you'd be working." She said, forcing a genial tone. Al had developed a habit of stopping by her home unannounced in the last month She resented his familiarity, but had not had the courage to tell him to knock it off.

"I have an appointment near here in a few minutes and decided to swing by," he said. Myra gave him a weak smile.

Look like you're interested. Be nice. "Who's the client?"

"A restaurant owner who wants to advertise his second location. The usual package. One of the easy ones. Another referral. Nice guy from Cleveland. He moved his family here last month. So," he said, drawing out his words. "I haven't heard from you in two weeks. What've you been doing?"

Myra's anxiety and resentment returned, but she caved at the wounded expression and eager eyes staring at her. His interest in her personal life annoyed her, but she put it down to his loneliness and boredom. She had to keep a professional rapport at the office. "Working, taking care of the house, walking Pepper, and reading. Boring, right?" Myra said.

"No, that's good. You need to get things done. How's it going at the office? I've been in the field a lot. "

"Fine. Nothing much changes there, but, you know me, I thrive on tediousness."

"Yes, I do know you."

Myra shuddered. She had run out of small talk and wanted to get back to her cozy corner to finish reading her book. They stood facing each other stuck for something to say. Myra moved her eyes to the neighbor across the street who walked out to his truck and waved at her. She returned wave and felt Al's eyes bore into her. Al had a creep factor she could not explain—an undercurrent that made her uncomfortable.

"Guess I'll get going. See you at the office," he said, and got in the car and turned on the ignition. He stared ahead for several seconds before turning back to Myra who now had shifted her attention across the street to a different neighbor whose children played with their new puppy in the front yard.

"Are you going to be home later?"

"Why?"

"What about meeting me for a drink later? I'll be keyed up after the meeting. It'll be nice to have company."

"I don't know."

"Come on. You're not busy."

"What makes you say that? I happen to have plans."

"What plans?"

"Thanks for the loan of the book, Al. Sorry I didn't return it sooner. Now, I have to get back inside. I'll see you at work."

Myra walked back inside, shut the door quickly, and turned the deadbolt. Leaning against the door, the sweat, the pounding in her ears, and quick breaths made it obvious to her she was afraid. Time to admit she had a problem.

She settled back in her recliner, feet up, delving back into the plot of her mystery with thoughts of Al far removed. Jon kept breaking into her thoughts through the mayhem on the pages. She smiled remembering their first meeting at her office when he came for an appointment with her boss. The thought of him made her ooze giddiness like a teenager. She giggled reliving the touch of his skin, his smell, and his deep green eyes so penetrating, she had to look away for fear of falling. She fake-fanned her neck before returning her attention back to murder. Deep into details of the murder room, she jumped as the telephone rang.

"Hey." Myra's heart raced hearing Jon's voice, sensual and commanding. "What's up? I called earlier but you didn't answer. I thought I'd invite myself over. Are you busy?"

"The words of a courteous man."

"What?"

"Well, I might as well tell you. Al stopped by again. This time to pick up the book he lent me. He invited me to meet him for a drink after his business appointments."

"Did you go?"

"Of course not. What do you think? I told him I had plans, thanked him for the book and rushed inside. I'm getting tired of him dropping by like that."

"He's interested in you, and for some reason, you're leading him to believe he's has a chance. At least, that's how he sees it."

"That's ridiculous. I'm trying to be nice. He's a coworker, that's all. How can he not know that," Myra said.

"Are you trying to convince me or yourself? Of course, you

might enjoy the attention. Maybe you're interested in him?"

"Now, you're stooping to manipulation."

"Realistic, you mean. You asked for trouble by not establishing boundaries from the start."

"I don't know what to do. He's someone I have to work with. Thank goodness, he's not in the office much, but I still have contact with him. What happens if I hurt his feelings?"

"He's nobody. A salesman and not even a top salesman. Handle the situation before it has a chance to turn ugly."

"What do you mean?

"Does he know about me?"

"No. You know we talked with my boss and we all decided to stay low-key. I haven't told anyone at the office."

"So he believes you're available. You're not, by the way," Jon said, lightening his tone. "I don't want you to be around unpleasantness if you don't need to. Find a way to tell him to stop dropping by. He should get the message."

"Get over here and help me figure it out."

"Be there in twenty."

Jon stepped onto the porch with an armful of food and wine.

"Hi, gorgeous girl," Jon said.

"Hi, handsome boy." Myra stood, her arms stretched across the doorway blocking his way. "Entry fee, one kiss."

"One will get you two," he said. Myra kissed him on both cheeks, then wrapped her arms around him and nipped his ear.

"No fair. Just wait until my arms are free."

After sorting out the Asian food boxes, pouring wine and settling in to watch a movie, they both jumped at a loud knock on the door. Both looked at the other, surprised at the interruption. "I guess I should see who it is," Myra said. She set down her wine glass and went to the front door.

"Al! What are you doing back here? You should have called first," said Myra, feeling Jon's eyes behind her.

"I finished the meeting and decided to stop by to see if

your plans changed." She saw Al try to look behind her, and at seeing a man's figure developed a hurt look on his face.

"I told you I had plans. I have company and don't have time to talk. You really should call before you drop in on someone." Between the wine and Jon's presence, Myra believed she had the courage to speak her mind.

"Sorry I bothered you. It won't happen again," Al said, red-faced and awkward. "I'll see you later," he said, turning and walked away. Myra watched him all the way to his car to be sure he left.

"Guess who that was?"

"Don't tell me. Al?"

"Can you believe he came back? Your car's right in front. You'd think he'd get a clue."

"He's more interested in you than you think. You won't get rid of him as easily as telling him you're busy."

Myra found Jon's directness an irritating trait, especially when he was right. Her face stung, and when her voice rose to that high, nasal pitch that signified her anger, she knew it was time to stop this conversation. How could she admit that she agreed with Jon, that she had felt anxious about Al's stop-and-go visits all along. He would tell her to listen to her inner voice more. Go with your gut. How could she explain that instincts had been unwelcome intrusions into her reality as far back as she could remember. Even as a child, she sensed her mother's moods on the walks home from school, knowing before she walked into the house that something bad was about to happen. Feelings she taught herself to stuff and ignore when they contradicted the reality she wanted. Crap, she thought, this situation is becoming uncomfortable. Admitting that Jon might be right was almost as bad as admitting it to him out loud. And letting those instincts run loose now made her afraid, because she sensed that Al was unstable.

"Okay Myra. We'll stop talking about it, but don't think it's over because you want to stop talking about it. He'll be back,"

"I'll say this," Myra said, forcing the calm back into her voice. "I've been nothing to Al but a co-worker, not even a friend. If he's made anything else of that, he has no one to blame but himself."

"That's going to be a matter of opinion. Just handle it soon. Set him straight before it goes too far. The longer you wait, the more time he has to think he has a chance."

"How did you get to be such a smart guy?"

"By paying attention," Jon said, reaching over to kiss her forehead and unfroze the television screen.

By the end of the movie, they were both laughing, joking, and playing, pushing Al's visit to the back of her mind, a vague and irrelevant incident

At her desk the next morning, rewinding her evening with Jon, she smiled as she turned on her computer screen to check for e-mails. Among the emails she expected every morning, she had an uneasiness seeing a message from Al from ten o-clock last night. She almost deleted it, but opened it in case it was business-related. As she feared, Al was asking her out for dinner. Deciding on the passive, non-confrontational approach, she wrote back, explaining that she was seeing someone now and would be having dinner with him. There. It's done. She brightened at the prospect that now she had told him, he would get it and leave her alone. She leaned back in her chair, and breathed out her relief.

Humming as she went, she filled her coffee mug and returned to her desk. Comfortable and ready to check the other emails, she heard a ding tone that told her she had a new message. Another message from Al. This was not good. She read "what about tomorrow?" Without greeting or salutation, she typed in capital letters the word "NO." Then, a third message asking for another evening. What will it take to get him to stop? She had to be blunt as much as she resisted the idea. Choosing her words, she wrote: "NO. Not going to happen. Stop harassing me. Learn to take no for an answer. And DO NOT drop by my house or call me at home again." She read it over two more times before pressing the send button.

Relieved she had put an end to that problem, she reached down into her desk drawer for her purse for her lip-gloss and hand mirror. Bent over the drawer, she noticed her hands shook as she ran the applicator over her lips. When she straightened upright, she heard Al speaking to her from the front of her desk,

"I guess this is a brush-off, then?"

"What are you talking about? You act as if we're dating. Are you nuts?" Myra said.

"What do you mean we're not dating? We've gone out several times and every time we did, I paid for your food or drinks. If that's not a date, I don't know what is."

Myra was speechless. She had to stall while she figured out what to say to him. His distorted features frightened her.

"Listen Al, I thought of you as a friend, a coworker, nothing more. I didn't say or do anything to give you the impression I was interested in a romantic relationship. You went to that place all on your own. You have no right to come in here in that threatening manner. "

"Who's this guy? How long has this been going on?"

"*He* is none of your business. I suggest if you're going to be unpleasant, you should leave my office now. I'm not going to discuss this with you anymore. Subject closed. Goodbye Al."

With all of the aggression she could invoke, Myra stared him down until he turned and walked away. Shaking from her hands to her knees, she sat down on her chair to get her bearings. She was grateful he worked in a different building. At least it was over.

That night, after three lengthy conversations with girlfriends on her harrowing experience of the morning, she leaned back in bed reading a P.D. James novel. Reading with relish the atmosphere in the death room and the explicit details of the condition of the corpse found with his throat cut, she jumped at a loud knock on the front door. Alert with the adrenaline rush, Myra sneaked into the living room without turning on the lights and peaked out through the front window. It was Al.

Damn. It's one in the morning. What does he want now? Pepper looked up at Myra, poised in attack mode next to her. Neither made a sound, human and animal understanding the need to be quiet. After the upsetting events of the morning, she decided there was no way she would answer him or open the door. Maybe he would think she was not home and go.

"I know you're in there, Myra. Open the door. I'm not leaving. We need to talk about this." Myra stood in the dark, frozen, listening to the pounding of her heart, her mouth dry, her knees growing weak.

"Alright, Myra. You win. But don't come crying to me later when he dumps you for someone else, because I won't have you. You're damaged goods."

Her body relaxed when she heard his footsteps walk away, followed his engine starting and the car moving out. When it sounded as if he were long gone, she rushed to the telephone to call her friend, Joanne, still too afraid to turn on the lights.

"Hello," said Joanne in a raspy groggy voice.

"Joanne, it's Myra. I'm sorry to call you this time of night, but I've just had the crap scared out of me by Al and I need to talk to someone."

"What the hell?" said Joanne, alert and concerned. Myra recounted the events of the last twenty-four hours, trying to remember each word in its proper sequence and tone.

"Call the police. You've got to stop this now."

"The police? Are you kidding me? Anyway, he said he was done with me. It's over. I just want to put this behind me."

"How naive you are, Myra. He's a nutter. You might think it's over, but it's not. Whackjobs don't walk away. You'll end up afraid of answering your own door or going out on your own. Sooner or later, he'll confront Jon, maybe attack him."

Myra listened. Joanne was speaking from personal experience from two years before. Joanne had more guts than she had, but still ended up in a brutal physical assault that ended in her shooting her ex-husband in the thigh. The police assumed she did not mean to mortally wound him, but she admitted later she aimed for his chest but had not yet learned to control the gun. Due to the restraining order and witness statements, she was not charged and he ended up going to prison. But she was not dealing with a jealous ex-husband. This was different. Right?

"Maybe he won't bother me again."

"Don't count on it. He's obsessive. Grow up. This is not a game."

"I should've said something when he first started stopping by my house. Of all the bad timing, to be harassed by a crazy man the same time I've met a great guy like Jon."

"Delusional types don't listen. I don't think saying anything would have changed the situation. Don't dwell on what you should've done. Plan on what you need to do for the future. "

"That'll be a first for me."

"Put a knife in your purse. That's easier and quieter than a gun."

"I can't do that."

"You're going to need a weapon when he attacks you. I'm bringing over my Walther. Just don't blow off your own foot trying to shoot him."

"No way. What makes you think he's going to physically attack me?"

"The crazy ones do that when they can't make reality fit their fantasies."

"I don't believe that."

"Do it anyway. Humor me. You can always tell me I was wrong, but you can't tell me I was right if you're dead. I'll be over first thing in the morning."

After two hours on the phone with Joanne, Myra calmed down enough to sleep. By this time, it was three o'clock, and she sank into a fast sleep, deep and regenerative after trauma. At five-thirty, Myra answered the insistent ringing coming from her cell phone with drowsy abandon. The ringing melded into the pleasant and warm environment of her dream's landscape, an annoyance but not a concern.

"Hello," Myra said, still more asleep than awake. The voice

of the caller thrust her thrust into a dark, ominous reality.

"Myra, this is Al. Why didn't you let me in last night? I wanted to talk about this and you behaved as if I was trying to come in to kill you. You hurt me. I don't understand your attitude." Today, the sound of his voice sounded sane and rational and Myra began to feel she imagined it all.

"If you think you can get rid of me that easily, you're mistaken. I won't stand for it. You hear me? We're not done until I say we're done."

"Leave me alone," Myra said into dead air. She pushed the phone to the edge of the night table. Her hands were shaking again. She tossed the covers across the bed before getting out of bed. Doing anything routine and mundane is what she needed right now. Pepper did his dance, spinning counter clockwise, and jumping at the sight of her picking up his food bowl. Dogs had a way of putting life in perspective. No problem more important than eating.

She made a strong cup of coffee and sat at the table to keep an eye on her breakfast. Holding the warm mug, she looked down onto the dark, thick liquid to watch the muted reflections from the overhead light until her movements caused the coffee to quiver inside the cup. She looked up to the window at the pre-dawn darkness and caught her image. She looked small, a bit disheveled, but cute, she thought, winking at her reflection in the window. She was a nice person. Why was happening to her? What cosmic forces played out here to taint her first good relationship?

When she heard the tapping on the window pane, she jumped. Joanne stood at the window, pink acrylic nails gently tapping on the glass.

"Come on. Open up," Joanne said.

Myra got up and unlocked the back door. "Sorry. I guess I was daydreaming."

"How nice to have lovely daydreams when your life is in danger."

Myra rolled her eyes, "Your sarcasm isn't wasted on me. He called at 5:30 and told me in so many words how right you are."

Joanne reached into her tote bag and pulled out a black gun and handed it to Myra. She thought how small and toylike it looks. Surely not a dangerous weapon.

"I thought it would be bigger,"

"It's only a twenty-two, but dangerous if you use it right."

Joanne showed her the safety and gave her brief instructions on how to hold the gun.

"I've got one in the chamber, so you're all set. Switch off the safety and pull the trigger. Keep firing until he's down."

"My God, Joanne. Isn't that excessive?"

"Listen. An old boyfriend who taught me to shoot said the first rule of fighting is never to turn your back on your opponent once you've injured him. If you give him the chance, he'll will come back at you and do to you what you thought you did to him."

Myra thought about a minute. Joanne was right, she thought. She could see a deranged person like Al was becoming, enraged and bent on revenge. "This is so messed up, Joanne. I'm scared."

"Victims are scared and helpless. Being a victim means he wins. Be a fighter instead and kick his ass."

Over dinner, Myra told Jon about Al's visit and phone call. Watching the distress on his face, she wished she had not told him anything.

"I'm sorry I wasn't there for you. You could've called me, you know. I would've come right over."

"I know, but it was late and I was embarrassed. You were right. I didn't handle the situation well and didn't want to create drama for you. No sense in both of us being upset. I admit, I had some tense moments, but it worked out."

"Promise me you won't try to be your own hero next time. I've grown accustomed to your face and would hate to lose you."

"I promise," Myra said. Behind her pleasant smile, she

thought of the gun next to bed and its empowering influence.

It was close to one o'clock when Jon left. Myra decided not to take him up on offer to stay with her. She reminded him that he had an early meeting and needed to focus. She omitted telling him that she felt invincible knowing she had the means to defend herself now. She had no idea what he thought about guns, much less a gun in the hands of an unskilled woman firing erratically at her attacker. There seemed to be a plethora of withheld information between couples owing to the fear of rejection or disapproval from the other. That justification eased the guilt of hiding the gun from him, but she would not turn back now.

By two o'clock, Myra had decided that Joanne had it wrong. Sitting in the dark since Jon left, she had stayed awake with the gun next to her on the night stand. Feeling safe, she slid under the covers and started to fall asleep.

A few minutes later, Pepper brought her back with a low warning growl. Myra sat up, listening. All she heard were the usual neighborhood sounds at first. She peeked out the window, but saw nothing unusual. She took the gun off safety, and started a slow walk to the kitchen to check out the back of the house.

Nothing looked disturbed. She heard Pepper growl again, and turned around to find a large figure of a man approaching her. He said nothing, but kept getting nearer. True fear had been a stranger to her until this second when the logical and irrational were the same. Her body tingling at its edges with a raw ache so primitive, there was nothing more important than living another minute.

When he was a stride away from her, she raised the gun and pulled the trigger. He kept coming, so she continued to fire until the magazine was empty. He still stood for several seconds before dropping to the floor.

"You didn't tell me you had a gun."

Myra recognized Jon's voice. Stricken that she had killed the wrong man, she flipped on the lights and rushed over to him.

"I thought you were Al. Why did you come back without telling me? I feel awful. I'll get my phone and call nine-one-one."

Before she moved away, he reached out to grab her hair and pulled her closer to him. Enduring the pain she thought he must be experiencing, he startled her when he reached her neck with both hands and started to squeeze. She fought him off and backed away, confused, but convinced he was angry that she shot him. She ran for her phone, explained the situation and the need for an ambulance.

When she turned around, Jon was on his knees trying to stand. Something different about him frightened her. Pepper had started to bark, backing away in fear as she did.

"Listen, Jon. I'm sorry I shot you. Joanne gave me the gun to protect myself against Al. I had no idea you were the one sneaking around in the dark. After all I told you, I can't believe you'd scare me like that. Please lie down. The ambulance will be here any minute."

"You ruined everything. Why couldn't you play the game the way you were supposed to?"

"What are you saying? I don't understand," Myra said. She backed up as he struggled to walk, his hands, once so gentle, now menacing, reached out for her.

She aimed the gun at him, still backing into the next room. He laughed, "I know the gun's empty."

He reached his right hand to his side and brought out a large hunting knife. The shiny surface seemed to glow in the dark kitchen.

"What are you doing with that?"

"What I came here to do," Jon reached up to take a swing at her when she heard a gurgle come from his throat and watched him drop to the floor. This time, he remained motionless. The quiet in the room hurt her head. Her shaking hands dropped the gun and she ran as fast as she could through the house to the front door where she ran into the arms of a policeman.

"I don't understand," Myra kept repeating to the officers.

"He said he came to kill me. What does it mean?" Someone wrapped her in a blanket and tried to quiet her.

"Do you have someone you can call?"

"Yes, my friend, Joanne."

"Give me her number and I'll call for you."

Myra still had her phone and handed it over. She had a blankness about her, confusion, weakness, unable to distinguish if she had just spoken to a man or a woman.

When she heard Joanne's voice, then a comforting embrace, she was able to cry. "Why did he want to kill me? I thought it was Al."

"It's a good thing you didn't know it was Jon or you might not be alive right now. Jon was not what he appeared to be. I think he was the guy who's been killing woman this past year, but the cops won't tell me anything."

Everyone turned to watch Myra as she burst into a hysterical laughter.

DOING THE TWIST

The Arizona sun burned through the metal bars of the window set high on the empty block wall of his cell. Stan Godbey contemplated the shadows on the concrete bench where he waited. His imprisonment in the Florence Prison was real, but after the trial, the verdict, and the pronouncement of the death penalty, he could not come to terms that this had happened to him.

He had read the transcripts that chronicled the courtroom proceedings, witness testimonies, and depositions of his social acquaintances and business associates. They painted a portrait of a despicable man who had swindled them and seduced the women in their lives under the guise of friendship. Stanley knew his arrest and subsequent background revelations had exposed them as gullible and vulnerable—their egos could not forgive him for that.

"The truly sad part of this case is that Godbey preyed on long-time friends," the prosecutor said. "He used those relationships and his victims' misplaced trust to commit his fraud, causing them emotional and financial hardship. But those crimes are for another court. But we have shown, ladies and gentlemen of the jury, that Stanley Godbey is a malignant narcissist and sexual predator, who ended the life of his perceived romantic rival for the sole purpose of acquiring financial gain for his girlfriend."

When the prosecutor announced that Stan was wanted in four states for questioning in the murders of four women last seen in his company, Stan's attorney had decided to alter his defense in favor of a clinical explanation for his behavior. Stan did not agree, but had to admit that being in the nuthouse was better than rotting on death row.

Stan's defense attorney argued that "Mr. Godbey has suffered from a congenital affliction since childhood called Mad King George's Disease, or Acute Intermittent Porphyria. All of the symptoms of this disease are psychiatric and manifest themselves during the toxic heme over-production that attacks his brain. Heme is an iron-rich enzyme. A person with this affliction loses control during these episodes, making him dangerous and violent while in this psychotic state. He should be institutionalized, not incarcerated, any more than we would jail an epileptic for a seizure." Stan thought that approach had been a mistake when combined with the other evidence and he found out he was right as the trial continued.

The prosecutor had destroyed Stan's meticulous reputation as a man of moral integrity when he revealed the details of his fraudulent land deals that had been perpetrated through his exaggerations and omissions of the truth. Those facts established his character.

The eyewitness accounts from the women in his life, past and present, had proven him a serial womanizer who controlled them through intimidation by verbal abuse and threats of violence. That established his inclination to violence.

The irony of his situation had not escaped him. The prosecutor had proven him to be a con man, guilty of numerous assaults against women, and suspected in several murders, but he had no real evidence for the present murder case. Stan believed he had been convicted by the momentum of the public disapproval and circumstantial evidence. He did not doubt he deserved punishment, but to be punished for the one murder he did not commit seemed a cruel twist of the knife.

His stomach fluttered with a nervous anticipation at hearing high heels striking the polished tile floor in the hall outside. One last visit by the woman he could always manipulate returned his sense of power. The heels stopped in front of his door, followed by a moment of stillness before he heard the click followed by the steel bar slide to the left that freed the door to swing open.

Carilyn ran to him and embraced him,. Her ashen blond hair up in a ponytail, swung back and forth around her long thin neck in time with her movements.

The guard watched them for several seconds. "Thirty minutes, ma'am," he said, and pushed the door closed.

"We've got to hurry, baby." Stan reached out for her waist to bring her toward him.

Carilyn leaned away and looked at him with unexpected indignation.

"Is sex all you think about, even at a time like this?"

"Well, we've got thirty minutes with unmonitored privacy. Why not? You're the one who set up this last meeting."

Her green eyes narrowed toward him with an expression he did not recognize. This docile creature that never stood up to him or questioned his actions seemed to have morphed into a different person since the trial. Was he at a disadvantage by his present situation, or was he seeing something that had been there all along? The reveal of the real woman behind the helpless feminine mask?

"I'll tell you why not. It's not going to happen now or ever again, at least not with me."

"Come on, baby. What's the matter with Daddy's little girl?"

"You're not my daddy and I'm not a little girl! I have something to tell you that I've wanted to say for a long time, so be quiet. It's a long speech."

"Oh, geez. Whatever," he shrugged. "Considering that

I'm due to die tomorrow, which one of your insignificant domestic crises could be so important?"

"Before you die, I want to be sure you know exactly why you're here."

Her chilly tone frightened him. Stan sat back on the concrete bench and watched her face.

"First, we want to thank you for providing us with the lovely money from Hank's life insurance policy. That $250,000 is going to make our lives so much easier. Without your conviction, the insurance company might have held up the payment while they kept investigating. Your lawyer called this morning to tell me you've named me in your will. Of course, there's not much left now after the legal fees, but thanks for that all the same."

"I did not kill Hank, so don't thank me."

"Well, you're the one being executed for his murder, aren't you?"

Stan thought he might strangle her if she did not stop talking. "Only because someone set me up."

"I've thought about everything you said to me over the years—that we'd get married and I could quit work to be a stay-at-home-mom again. But guess what, that never happened. Don't think I've forgiven you for that."

"I've heard all this before. So what?"

She ignored him. "All those speeches about taking care of me and my kids. How you'd always be by my side no matter what. How I would never have to worry about anything ever. All lies! My friends tried to tell me. My parents tried to tell me. Dammit, my kids even tried to tell me. I kept telling them that if he *weren't* going to marry me, why else would he keep hanging around. You made a fool out of me. Not only that, but you wasted my time when I could have found someone else."

Carilyn paused. She was shaking.

Stan had the overwhelming urge to infuriate her. "Oh good, you stopped talking. Or did you just come up for air?"

He had always enjoyed belittling women. This *was* his last chance, after all. "Is it my fault that you invented this fairytale? I never said I'd *marry* you and live in the same house with all those children. What I said was I would *take care* of you if you needed my help. Friends with benefits."

He knew she wanted to hit him, but she stayed standing in the middle of the room. "So you think twisting words to suit you makes it okay. You didn't have to actually say the words for me to get your meaning."

"I'm not responsible for what you *think* is supposed to happen. Don't make yourself a victim. I did plenty for you and you know it."

"It doesn't matter. Not now anyway," Carilyn said. She shrugged and started to circle the small room, heels clicking hard on the bare concrete floor causing a harsh echo. She spun around toward him, and said, "You think I didn't believe Sheila, don't you?"

"You're not bringing her into this again, are you?" Stan shifted on the bench, and snarled up at her.

"I pretended to believe you because I thought there was still a chance I could get what I wanted for me and my kids. I thought she was standing in the way of you marrying me. Boy, was I ever an idiot. "

"You're an idiot for ever believing anything she said. She wanted me, too, and invented a relationship that never happened. I told you that."

"Practically at death's door and you're still a liar. I don't think you know what the truth is. You would say anything to anyone to get your way."

"You drove all the way down here to whine?"

"No, I drove all the way down here to tell you that you've been screwed—royally. And there's nothing you can do about it."

"What's that supposed to mean?"

Carilyn lowered her voice, leaned over, and spoke into his ear, "We did it. We set you up."

Stan watched her laugh.. The expression on her face and the sound of the words she said paralyzed him. Was she serious? For the first time since he could recollect, he had lost control—sucker punched and breathless. He wanted to talk, but nothing came out. His heart pounded in his ears. He gasped, but his chest tightened and blocked his air.

"You were right about my ex-husband. A loser from the day I married him. If I'd realized it then, I'd never have had those kids. It was bad enough that he couldn't hold down a decent job, but then he started doing drugs, like we could afford that. His parents wouldn't help us, and they should've—he was their only child. My folks wouldn't help either. They just kept telling me they'd babysit while I worked. Like me working answered all the problems. The only decent thing my ex ever did was to take out that insurance policy. I made sure I paid the premiums, even after the divorce."

She stopped pacing. Her eyes looked wild, glazed over as if she were witnessing an invisible scene. "But you probably want me to get to the good part. Just so you know, I never liked the way you treated my children—ridiculing them, harassing them, and trying to pretend they weren't there. I might not have cared for my ex, but that didn't give you the right to judge him. Who are you to think you're so much better when you've had everything and have only ever thought of yourself. It's all that mocking and viciousness that gave us the idea."

"Us? You mean the kids were in on it?"

"No. Us as in Sheila and me. You were so busy working on isolating everyone, you weren't paying attention. I was angry at Sheila as long as I believed she threw herself at you all the time. The day I realized she was telling the truth was when I found your letter to another woman complaining about me. You had the nerve to reveal my personal business to another woman while telling her how you enjoyed your time with *her* between the sheets. That's when I knew what a liar you are."

"But that was five years ago. You kept hanging on to that?"

"You want to know the most irritating thing about you? It's that habit you have of minimizing everyone's feelings. No humility. No empathy. Never accepting responsibility for hurting people, just deflecting all the blame onto the other person."

Stan opened his mouth to protest, but Carilyn held out her hand and said, "Don't even speak. I can't stand to listen to another word. I'll just tell you this last thing. Your arrogance was easy to use against you. You had to tell everybody how much better you were than my ex-husband and how my kids would be better off if he were dead. Look at all the witnesses at the trial who testified about what you said. Even my children told how you picked on their dad. Your delusion that you're superior over the proletariat made the story believable." She started to laugh. Her eyes frightened him—glassy and distant. She paused, took a deep breath, and then looked back to him.

"I bet you still can't figure out why Sheila didn't admit to calling you that night. Pleading for you to rescue her on that isolated road outside of town. She couldn't admit that in court, because that was part to our plan. She used Hank's phone to call you. We knew you're too cheap to have caller ID on your home phone and wouldn't know one call from another. She called you from the same area as Hank's body to put you on the scene and make sure you didn't have an alibi. You see, I shot Hank before she made the call, and still got home in time to have an alibi from my *adoring* parents. Sheila practiced the timing for weeks. The hot rocks under the thin mattress kept his body warm long enough to make it appear he died at the time you had no one to confirm your whereabouts." This time, she looked him directly in the eyes with a level of rage that Stan had never encountered before.

"I think she and I made a pretty good team, both of us

knowing you so well. You were predictable. It's funny in a way. You thought you were so untouchable that you believed you would never be convicted. Maybe if you hadn't been so confident that the jury would believe you, you might have spent more time figuring out who framed you. At first, the prosecutor looked at me as the person with the best motive, but your attorney painted me as the good-hearted woman—the victim of unfortunate circumstance, kind and gentle soul. By the time the prosecutor got done with you, even Sheila looked like a victim of your maliciousness instead of a co-conspirator in the murder. It couldn't have been written better."

"You bitch. You think you're going to get away with this? As soon as you leave, I'm calling my lawyer," he said. Stan lunged for her but missed when she stepped aside.

She had the nerve to laugh at him again. "No one can prove anything. It'll be a last desperate ploy from a pathetic loser to save his sorry ass."

"I'll tell him about the rocks."

"So what? Rocks are everywhere on the desert floor. You won't win even if someone gets suspicious. There's no evidence anywhere that Sheila and I ever spoke or ever met, except for five years ago. With your reputation, who'll believe a word you say. I think they called you a sociopath in court. I wish I had seen that before. I guess I wish a lot of things," she said.

"Guard!" she yelled out and pressed the red button beside the door. Within seconds, the key turned in the lock, and the metal bar slid to release the door.

Before walking through the threshold, Carilyn looked back at Stan, her face expressionless and cold, "Bye, darling. Good luck in the next life."

Every nerve in his body burned. He stood there, wanting to yell out for help, but his face became numb. His mouth formed words but gibberish came out. He looked for something nearby to hold onto but weakness dropped him to the floor. He had no feeling in his body. He could not move from the uncomfortable position or use his throat to push out words to call for help.

The guards found him and rushed him to the prison hospital. The doctors said he had had a watershed stroke. Stan closed his eyes and recalled the words he had heard when they thought he was not aware.

"The poor bastard will miss his execution tomorrow, but he won't enjoy it. We know he can hear us but he'll never speak or use most of his body again. Sounds like there is a God after all."

Carilyn smiled as she drove from Butte Avenue to Highway 87, and then continued west until she spotted the rest area. She pulled into an empty parking space, switched off the radio, and took a long drink of water from the bottle tucked between the front seat and the cup holder. The place looked deserted, and she became annoyed that she had to wait until she saw the familiar sedan pulling in from the opposite direction. She smiled, removed her seatbelt, and got out when the other car pulled in next to hers.

"So, how did it go?"

"It went better than you could imagine. Too bad you missed that priceless expression on his face when I told him everything."

Sheila grinned, "It's what he deserves."

"That's my take on it. Listen, I brought you some cash to hold you over until the insurance money comes through," Carilyn said.

"Great, but I told you I would wait. No sense in raising red flags by taking out large sums of money."

"Don't worry about that. You took a lot of risks to help me. You had no financial motive, and I appreciate what you've done for me. It's in the trunk," Carilyn said, waving her index finger toward the back of the car. "I'll pop it open for you."

Sheila turned her back on Carilyn to walk to the back of the car. Before she had taken three steps, Carilyn pulled out a hammer from under her car seat and let the hammerhead bear down on Sheila's skull.

She watched Sheila collapse like a marionette. Carilyn was stunned by Sheila's black hair floating down around her head into a feather-like formation on the ground.

"Dumb bitch."

Carilyn checked her clothes and her car for blood, wiped off the hammer with paper towels, and tossed both into the trash barrel. She looked around one more time, grateful for the isolation of the spot. She drove to Interstate 10, then headed back to Phoenix, putting distance between her and the unpleasantness of the incident with Sheila. The episode played like someone else's dream.

The next morning, Carilyn woke to a sunny, cool morning, feeling lighter than she had since she had been a child. Even the bickering among her children and the chaos of the dogs competing for food and human attention did not aggravate her as they had yesterday. The world had become a wonderful place of endless opportunities. Her life was about to change forever.

She watched the morning news flash that Stanley's execution had been indefinitely postponed due to the severe stroke he suffered yesterday afternoon. *Can my day get any better?* But the top news story was "an unrelated murder with a tragic twist. Sheila Brighton, one-time girlfriend of convicted murderer, Stan Godbey, was murdered at a rest stop not far from the prison."

Carilyn sipped her coffee after the children had gone to school, and envisioned her plans for the insurance money. Idyllic settings where she lounged on the beach in a faraway place with a drink and a cool ocean breeze played over in her head until her head swam. The telephone rang and interrupted her thoughts. She frowned, reached for the cordless, and pressed the talk button.

"Carilyn, this is Detective Macy. We met during your ex-husband's murder investigation."

"Oh, yes. I remember you. How are you?"

"Fine, thank you. I wondered if I might stop by. Something has come up that I need to speak to you about. Are you available now?"

Hearing the casual tone in the detective's voice, Carilyn had no reason to worry. "Come as you like," she said.

Five minutes late, Carilyn jumped at the sound of the doorbell. Detective Macy and another man stood on the other side of her front door.

"You're quick. Come in. Would you like a cup of coffee?"

"No thank you. As I said, something has come up that concerns you."

"You look serious, Detective."

"This is a serious business, Carilyn. I'll get straight to the point. I'm sure you've heard on the news this morning that Sheila Brighton was murdered yesterday."

"Yes, I just heard it on the television," Carilyn said.

"We're not sure who killed her. Not yet, anyway, but she left a letter that was to be opened in the event of an untimely death."

"How odd of her," she said.

"In this letter, she claims the two of you designed a plan to kill your ex-husband and frame Stan Godbey. She wrote that she wanted revenge, but that your motive was the insurance policy money."

"That's ridiculous. I wouldn't have had anything to do with that tramp after what happened. She's a liar. I'm the real victim here. Why can't you see that?"

"Not only does she give details of your meetings, and how you two accomplished the murder and set up Godbey, but she also wrote that she was to have a final meeting with you yesterday at the exact spot where she was killed. She said she wrote all of this down because she wasn't sure you could be trusted. That you weren't just using her until you received the money. She said if you turned on her, she wanted to make certain the authorities knew what happened. To that end, she had another letter addressed to the insurance company."

Carilyn broke out in a sweat and began to shiver.

"This is nonsense. Nobody can prove any of this. How can someone get away with writing a letter like that and have it taken seriously?"

"You'd better lock up the house and get your things. You'll be coming with us."

"Oh, no," Carilyn remembered saying before she fainted. What she did not remember saying after that was, "After all my planning."

HEAVY MASCARA

ABOUT THE AUTHOR

Cathy Ann Rogers has a penchant for creating literary characters who imitate reality through their skewed sense of justice as well as their bittersweet victories.

Cathy attributes the shaping of her writer's prowess to her solitary upbringing as an only child. Armed with a library card from her neighborhood branch in Cincinnati, she spent her childhood absorbed in suspenseful scenes depicted within the fiction of Christie and Conan-Doyle. Simultaneously, she built a mental library of potential plots while eavesdropping on the conversations of adults who discussed everything from Hollywood to History. The result of these blended influences is her fascination with plot twists and multi-generational storytelling in novels.

Following the dictates of her left-brain, Cathy pursued a degree and graduate certificate in accounting, establishing a tax and bookkeeping service for entrepreneurs. However, she maintained her right-brain passion for storytelling and puzzle solving. She sees a correlation between the discerning pertinent records from the irrelevant in accounting to assembling clues to solve a mystery. Both require the organization of information for a final solution.

Following the publication of her first novel, *Here Lies Buried*, Cathy brought life to this retrospective collection of new and previously-published short stories written over the last twenty years. She is currently working on the other writing projects due to appear before 2015.

Cathy weaves her tales from her Arizona desert townhome in the company of her Bichon Frises, Whitney and Sophie.

www.ingramcontent.com/pod-product-compliance
Lightning Source LLC
Chambersburg PA
CBHW030230180626
46810CB00008B/3065